To/ Cath & Bump

Congratulations!
Thanks for all the fantastic support and fun in Outpatients!

Lots of Love

Harvey

Toni x

The Farthing and The Devil

TC Harvey

AuthorHouse™ UK
1663 Liberty Drive
Bloomington, IN 47403 USA
www.authorhouse.co.uk
Phone: 0800.197.4150

© 2015 TC Harvey. All rights reserved.

No part of this book may be reproduced, stored in a retrieval system, or transmitted by any means without the written permission of the author.

Published by AuthorHouse 04/08/2015

ISBN: 978-1-5049-4013-9 (sc)
ISBN: 978-1-5049-4014-6 (hc)
ISBN: 978-1-5049-4015-3 (e)

Print information available on the last page.

Any people depicted in stock imagery provided by Thinkstock are models, and such images are being used for illustrative purposes only.
Certain stock imagery © Thinkstock.

This book is printed on acid-free paper.

Because of the dynamic nature of the Internet, any web addresses or links contained in this book may have changed since publication and may no longer be valid. The views expressed in this work are solely those of the author and do not necessarily reflect the views of the publisher, and the publisher hereby disclaims any responsibility for them.

Dedication

This book is dedicated to:

My Family,

My friends,

And all those who love to write.

Acknowledgements

First and foremost I wish to thank Janet, without whom, this book would never have been written. I then need to thank Penny, for getting it past the first few chapters, and then a massive thank you to all my friends, family and fellow writers who have supported me.

To my editor, Rachel, thank you for your unending help and all the work you put into this book.

To my friends that make up Penstraze Writers; Amy, Janet, James and Bee, you have been amazing!

To my mum, my dad, my brother and sister, thank you. Thank you for the unfaltering support and words of encouragement during yet another of my insane endeavours.

Lastly, thank you to my other half, Gino. You have been by my side every step of this journey and have always been there and kept me going.

Thank you x

Prologue

I hear a distant scream echo through the village. It is the call of the tribal leader, signalling the start of the Voodoo ceremony. As his scream cuts off others mirror his primitive cry. The drums begin; a slow steady beat that calls through the torrid air. Others join the cause, beating their drums in unmelodious harmony. The distant beat grows stronger as they dance through the dusty streets.

Soon the drums surround my hut, pounding through the earthen walls, beating their indelicate rhythm into my battered soul. My eyes flicker open, coming to rest upon the last rays of a blood-red sun flaming through a glassless window, the dancing men casting ferocious forms on the cobwebbed wall.

Tribal men call to Fa as women sing. I can feel hundreds of bare feet pound sun seared ground as they dance, the fever spilling out to the masses; the dry taste of tainted is earth thick in my mouth from upturned soil. I place my hands upon the rough table and feel the vibrations singing through the wood, my cup of water a mass of ripples fighting for escape in the fevered festival.

The crowd are screaming, chanting their words to the heavens. The drums grow louder and faster as the tribes meet, the dancing becoming frenzied as the Voodoo Spirit's take possession of their souls. I hear a howl spring from amid the crowd as flames consume wood, the smell of blazing timber overwhelming the stench of dry earth and hot human odour. The flames lash their shadows against the wall, throwing the forms of painted men into sharp relief as they dance amid the setting sun.

I cautiously make my way to the ornate, out of place, cabinet that has been pushed against the far wall. How had it come to be here? I wonder idly as I run my forefinger over the intricately carved wood that had once been polished to a high finish. Slowly my hand falls to the cool brass handle. My hand stills, for a moment, before dragging the draw open with an echoing groan that is lost amid the frenetic rhythm.

It is where I left it. The dark leather shines softly in the light from the blaze outside; for me it holds so many secrets; so much history.

I gently lift the book from its shadowy confines and carry it back to the table. I take my time, first setting down a cloth so as not to damage the leather on any unseen splinters of wood, before laying open the book. I light the old tarnished candelabrum that is sat atop the dresser and place it in the centre of the table. Pulling open another draw I take out my dip pen and ink.

I walk back to the table and sit, carefully, deliberately. I pull the candelabra closer, until I can see the page clearly. With the drums infecting me, pushing me on, I place pen to parchment.

I begin to write.

Chapter 1

I was staring through the grimy window of a chemist's shop. I could see minute spots of dirt that had clung to imperfections in the glass giving life to blisters of fungi. The window was encased in crystals of ice that had formed around its edges. Casting my eyes up the street I admired the frozen iron brackets that decorated the shops. In summer they would be full of flowers, flowing like vibrant juices from elaborate baskets. For now they held glittering stalactites, reaching their tenuous limbs towards the frosty ground.

I took the corner of my torn shirt and rubbed an area of glass free from frost as fresh snow settled on my numbed hands. Disregarding the cold I took my time to examine the trinkets on display in the window. There were glass jars stoppered with cork, offering protection from typhoid, influenza, scarlet fever and whooping cough. Each label had been carefully hand written in elaborate black lettering. I knew one of these potions would save my sister but it was only the rich who could afford such luxuries. Behind the miracle cures were many more charm boxes and bottles, all cleaned to a sparkling finish. On the shelf above were three vast jars. The first contained a thick crimson liquid; the second, an emerald green potion; the third was like looking into a beautiful blue haze. I could have stayed for hours, examining the tiny chests, pretty wrappings and extravagant lotions.

Looking past the window dressing I gazed in awe as a woman glided past in a handsome dress. The deep purple, tightly-fitted bodice had black flowers lovingly embroidered into the soft material. The stems flowing up from her waist curved into beautiful bouquets around her cleavage, exaggerating her shapely proportions. A full skirt fanned from her waist with banks of fabric flowing out behind her.

As she floated past I caught a glimpse of the proprietor in the window. The look in his eye was certainly not a welcoming one. I stood frozen, not from cold but dread, my encrusted toes curling in anticipation of what was about to befall me. The manager stormed through the door and advanced. I shrunk back, lifting my hands instinctively to protect myself.

"Get out of here kid. Go on, GO!" he shouted, hand high in warning. Striding towards me he pushed me further into the main street and into oncoming carriages.

Stumbling away from him I barely missed a dray as the shire horses pulling it thundered past at a vigorous trot, the barrels of beer it was carrying dancing precariously upon its bare boards. I quickly scurried to the other side of the immaculate street.

I ran through the town, my bare feet slapping painfully on the hard cobbled path. Rounding a corner too fast I tripped, skidding to my knees on the rough stones. Rolling over I clutched the hand that had broken my fall. As I slowly pushed myself up, bent double and sucking the air through my clenched teeth, I saw I had ripped my skirt. The dull, tattered fabric now bore a tear to the knee.

I dragged myself to my feet and stumbled down the alley, looking behind to check I was not being followed. I made my way into the narrow back alleys, only wide enough for one person to walk, my path hindered by rubbish, rubble and beggars. I struggled on as I stepped over a mutilated boy, an old tin rattling in his dirty hand. He turned his face towards me as I stepped over his bare legs, his blue toes brutally cut and infected. His eyes scarcely opened as he squinted up at me; a gleam of white cloudy eye staring blindly.

"Any change for the poor?" he asked as I stumbled over him.

"Sorry, no money to give," I muttered as I averted my eyes. I had seen this too many times before; a family mutilating their own child for monetary gains was nothing new here.

I looked to the end of the ally, towards home and my ailing sister, surprised to see the sun sinking behind the buildings. I had lingered too long. A ripple of fear ran through my body. Grace had looked so frail when I left this morning. Her hands trembling as I held her before leaving, her knuckles bulging and white through her thin, paper-like skin.

I kept my head down, my eyes on the cobblestones as I ran back to the main street, making my way back to Devils Acre. The shops began to get smaller and more dilapidated the closer I got to home. I looked down the sullied street and studied the innate differences. The uneven path was covered in semi-frozen pools of excrement, the smell of human waste and rotting substances stinging my nostrils, the smell sticking to the inside of my mouth.

A starving dog was digging through a mound of waste that was piled high by the side of a rundown house. I could see a small child edging closer, gauging the dog's reaction. As he took another tentative step forward the dog turned, his lips curling back to show his teeth. A menacing growl rose from deep in its throat. The child quickly backed away, lowering his body in submission.

I turned away, not wanting to come to the dog's attention. Dashing to the other side of the street I walked behind a textile stall. The rags were hanging in untidy rows. They ranged from complete shirts to nothing more than squares of cloth that could be used to patch existing garments.

The owner of the stall glared at me. He was leaning heavily on the side of his stall, each small shuffle costing him great pain, his rheumatic joints swollen and disjointed in the cold. He grimaced again as he tried to lean his weight on his bad leg, gripping the edge of the stall to keep himself standing. I was hedging my bets when I saw the cane leaning next to him. In a moment of surprising agility he grabbed the stick and took a swing through the air.

"Don't even think about it," he snarled.

I quickened my pace, skirting around the crowd until I was out of sight. I did not want my face remembered; it may hinder any future opportunities. It is not that I condoned thievery but this was the poorest area of London;

every crevice and sewer crawled with the diabolical life of the London slums. To live, you first had to survive.

Eventually I passed the brothel at the end of my road. A girl, three years older than me at most, was stood outside. Her grey, spoiled was dress pulled low across her chest with her ruined skirt gathered high above her knee in a bony hand. Leaning against the wall she watched me as I walked past, blowing smoke from a grimy cigarette dispassionately through her thin lips. I could smell cheap liquor, mingled with the smell of tobacco smoke and body odour as it flowed pungently through the open back door. I listened to laughing and singing and the sound of a piano being clumsily played as I walked past. Light was filtering through the windows from the low slung oil lamps. The light would flicker and dim as people danced past, the women giggling as they were taken around the room by a man paying for the privilege.

I was walking past the window when I heard a crash from within. A woman screamed as the piano cut off abruptly. I quickened my pace as I came around the front of the building, not wanting to find myself in the middle of a street brawl.

Just as I was going to step past the front door two men came hurtling through it. The small man on top looked to be the doorman. The other may have been bigger, but was at the distinct disadvantage of lying on his back with his trousers around his knees. Looking down I realised it was Ned. He lived in the same building as me. He had once been a good man but soon after arriving he had turned to drink and trying his luck at the local brothels.

Evidently, tonight his luck had run out. His smallpox-scarred face was contorted in drunken rage. Incoherent with alcohol and anger Ned seemed past all reason.

The smaller man was in the process of shouting at Ned, "you can't touch what you can't afford. And just to make it clear, you ca…a…afff….." at this point he realised his mistake. He had put himself nose to nose with Ned to make his point. He was then greeted with a vice like grip wrapped around his neck, Ned's large hands squeezing his windpipe, cutting off his vital supply of air.

The doorman was scratching at Ned's face, his nails digging into the delicate skin under his eyes. I could see blood beginning to pool at the indentations of his fingers. As Ned applied more pressure the man's hands clawed down his cheeks, followed by streaks of dark red blood. He was trying to roll off Ned, his legs flailing in vain. In a last effort the doorman pounded on Ned's chest and tore at his hands, his feet losing their purchase on the ground.

I could see this was getting out of hand. Ned, normally a pleasant man, would soon find himself in the gallows if he did not stay his attack. I leant down and whispered in his ear, "Ned, Ned. Come on. It's time to come home now."

His eyes slowly swung towards me.

"It's late and I'm scared to walk home by myself, will you help me?"

I glanced at the doorman. He was foaming at the mouth, the blood vessels in his eyes beginning to burst. I placed my hand on top of Ned's and rubbed his fingers gently. As his grip began to loosen the man dragged in a gratefully-received gulp of air. Finally Ned released his grip. The doorman sat back on his haunches before falling back, his chest heaving, his limbs convulsing with the lack of oxygen.

Rather than stay for the eventual fall-out I thought it best to get Ned home. Hauling him to his feet I took one last glance at the doorman, he had stopped shaking, but was still taking great efforts to draw the air into his lungs. I looked around; nobody seemed inclined to stop us so I began staggering with Ned down the street.

"Swa' worth it, ya' know," he drawled drunkenly.

I stifled a giggle. "What was worth it?"

"That bit o' a mis'undr'stand'in. She was some good lookin'. To be 'onest, I couldn't help m' self," he slurred incomprehensibly, his accent harder to understand than usual.

It had taken me a long time to get used to the odd way he spoke, rolling his R's and the strange lilt he gave to certain letters. I now know where that came from; those dark days in Africa had been short lived, but had left their mark. His life before Devils Acre was a mystery to most, and now I know why.

I looked up at him, he seemed proud of himself, for whatever he felt he had achieved that evening. He reminded me of my father. He had been a bit rough around the edges, and maybe not the best influence on me with regards to being light-fingered, but he was steadfast and reliable.

My father had assured us that he was leaving to earn more money. There was a job far away, somewhere, he never told us where. He said he would send us money, saving the rest until one day he would come back, taking us to a big family home that he would have bought with his riches.

That was the last time I had seen or heard from my father. It was only me, my sister Grace and my mother now. We lived with other families, but they had no help to offer, overburdened with their own difficulties. Ned would always lend an ear but he was in no fit state to offer any real assistance. More often than not it would be us caring for him.

Shivering, we finally made it to the front door. I managed to miss the stream of faeces that ran in front of our home. Ned unfortunately did not. He stepped in the middle of the revolting pool, splashing it up his legs. As he toppled through the door I had no choice but to let him go. He fell, face first, not bothering to raise his hands to protect himself.

I clambered over his body to assess the damage to his head, my frozen feet struggling to find their footing. He had smashed his nose. It had a slight crook to the left and blood was streaming from both nostrils. Fortunately he did not seem perturbed by these events. Trying to wipe the blood away from his nose his fingers fumbled uselessly, repeatedly missing his face.

He tried to push himself up, but with much groaning and griping he soon gave it up as a lost cause. All I could do was coax him further into the house at a crawl.

Ned currently stayed in a room down from ours. He had no living quarters of his own but normally found the most clean and comfortable part of the Brewers' floor. Tonight he settled for under their kitchen table. Adam Brewer had taken Ned in some time ago. I had recently noticed the two of them had become inseparable. I had caught them skulking about the alleys behind the house and heard them having discrete conversations behind closed doors, their secret words indiscernible in the din of so many in such a confined space.

It took some time, and a certain level of persuasion, but eventually I managed to get Ned onto a chair. There was an old man, evidently a new resident, slumped on the floor snoring heavily and two children were playing in front of the empty hearth. I shooed the children away with a steely glare and threw a moth eaten blanket over the drunk before gently mopping the blood from Ned's face with an old rag.

"Thanks Clara. You take good care o' me. O' all o' us. You need t' care for yourself too ya' know." The blood trickling over his lips caused the words to blur into one another. Despite this I could see the sincerity burning behind his eyes.

I pressed the bloodied rag into his hand and turned to leave.

"Good night Ned, and may god bless you while you sleep," I whispered, as I kissed him on his cheek.

"God bless ya' Clara."

I smiled down at him, knowing my lifted cheeks hid none of my sadness, before softly closing the door as I left.

I begrudgingly made my way across the noisy corridor, picking my way through the mass of bodies. The house was teeming, with the constant loss and gain of life the number of inhabitants in the building was changeable almost daily. I had left this morning with the cries of a woman as she watched her husband slip away, accompanied by the shrieks of a girl bringing a new life into our ungodly world. I wondered if, in these noxious times, the mother had survived her first day, or for that matter, if the baby had. My mind was drawn back to my sister; dread crept over me like a poison eating away at my flesh.

Finally I came to our room. As I stepped into our area of the house I glanced around to see what needed to be done. It was evident that my mother had been caring for Grace all day and the dirt floor was covered in a sticky residue that smelt all too familiar. I got a bucket of water from the side and sloshed it over the floor; we had a spare pail that would see us through until morning and something had to be done. I fetched the broom and started brushing the filth towards the drain in the corner. It was not clean, but it was better than it had been.

Our table held nothing but a wash basin full of dirty water; I slopped it out of our tiny window, tucked in the chair and surveyed the rest of the room. It seemed to be in fairly good order. Our plates, cooking pan and the few utensils we owned were where I had left them. There was no fire burning which meant that not only had my family not eaten, but also that we would be unlikely to eat tonight.

I walked to our sleeping area where Grace was lying on our bed. I could see a layer of sweat covering her body. Mother was using rags soaking in a pail of water to wet her skin, desperately trying to cool the fever.

I moved to her side as I asked the unnecessary question: "How is she?"

My mother could not answer. It was obvious she was getting worse. I crouched down beside my sister and studied her. Her cheek bones protruded from the sides of her face making her look grotesque. Her unfocussed eyes wandered around the room. I questioned whether she could see anything but the images conjured by her mind. She was moaning and grabbing at her stomach, pulling at her sweat-sodden shirt.

I held her hand; tears spilling from my eyes as I tried to offer her comfort. I hardened my grip as another seizure took her, a forsaken moan escaping her lips as her movements became wilder. She pulled against me. Suddenly her eyes focussed on the wall. Her face contorted into an image of fear as her bottom jaw quivered. She started screaming, writhing on the bed, before falling to the floor. I tried to keep hold of her but her strength reared from some deep, unknown place in her body; somewhere borne from fear. She thrashed and kicked, digging her fingernails into the grime covered floor. Her breathing became fast and shallow, her eyes beginning to swim. Her strength left her as quickly as the fear had taken her. She collapsed in a heap, her small chest heaving with the effort she had made to escape her imaginary foe.

My eyes stung with tears as I looked down at Grace. To see what she had been reduced to was too much for me to bear. I could not meet mother's eye. I shook the tears from my face as I pushed myself up.

"I don't think she's doing so well," I said. I had nothing left to give, had no comfort to offer my mother.

"She's just a bit hot is all; she'll be all right come morning. Won't you Grace?" My mother's convictions may have sounded convincing but I could see her hands shaking as she changed the rags for cooler ones. "You couldn't get the fire going? The wood looks a little damp," she added, her eyes never moving from her eldest daughter.

As night fell I could hear Grace coughing again. She was worse than an hour ago. As my numbed fingers again dropped the matches, the small splinters of wood scattering across the dirty floor, my hands fell to my knees, my head bowed in defeat. I stared into the darkness, a solitary salty tear running down my grubby cheek as I tried to remember the girl my sister had been. I wished I could hear her laugh one more time. I remember, years ago now, before even father left, the two of us playing scotch-hoppers. Grace had picked up a piece of coal from the cold hearth and dragged me excitedly from the house.

We ran through the streets hand in hand, oblivious to the world around us. When we got to a fairly unpopulated area Grace painstakingly drew out connecting squares using the coal.

"Hold on, we need something to throw," she called distractedly as she ran to a nearby house, picking up a small pebble before skipping back to me, her hands swinging in great arcs of childish pleasure.

"You first Clara," Grace had said, pressing the smooth black pebble into my palm. "Throw it," she insisted pointing to the network of squares.

I tossed the rock, watching as it scuttled across the uneven ground, coming to rest in one of the roughly drawn squares.

"Now what do I do?" I had asked, unable to stop giggling.

"You hop and jump down the squares," she laughed, hopping down the line, "but you have to miss the square you marked," she said, stooping to pick up the stone before jumping over the square and continuing to the end.

She got back to me and threw the stone again.

We played for hours, scotch-hopping our way up the street. As I danced over the squares Grace sang to me.

"What's your favourite?" Grace asked, stopping mid song.

"Sing a song of Sixpence."

With a smile Grace began to sing.

As she drew breath to finish the song we heard a familiar voice singing from behind us.

"They sent for the king's doctor,

Who sewed it on again;

He sewed it on so neatly,

The seam was never seen."

I looked up to see our father walking towards us, singing the last verse with gusto.

"Father!" we had exclaimed. Immediately forgetting our game we ran up to him, throwing our arms around his neck as he lifted us high in the air. Laughing, he spun us in a wide circle, clutching us close to his chest.

For one glorious minute I could hear my sisters laugh, feel the sun on my skin, the love of my father as he held us. I blinked, bringing myself back to my sister's fate, back to the cold, back to the darkness.

I could hear the rattle of her chest, her body struggling to take in a morsel of air. The house was dark, a cold mist hung in the air, seeping into my soul, infecting my hearts relentless beats with the pounding inevitability of death. I could no longer see the stack of twigs I was attempting to light, had no feeling left in my fingers. With a sob of defeat I abandoned my fruitless efforts and huddled next to the wall. Closing my eyes, I eventually fell into an uneasy sleep, my last thought: I could not lose her.

I awoke the next morning to a white frost covering our floor and my mother crying softly; the cold night had ended my sister's desperate struggles.

I felt hollow, like a part of my heart had been ripped away, discarded to the forgotten lands. My mother and I sat for hours, just looking at each other, trying to offer comfort yet not being able to comfort ourselves.

Ned disposed of her body. We had no money to pay for her burial and cremation was a desecration of the body and soul. He carried her to the graveyard late that evening, placing her in a grave dug for a funeral the following day. He shovelled just enough earth over Grace to cover her corpse. As the sun rose she would be put to rest, the mourners unaware that they were lamenting more than one body that day.

That morning mother and I walked to the graveyard with Ned. The silence surrounding us was deafening, like a cold wind raging against my raw soul. Stood at the entrance we looked on as unknown mourners surrounded the grave site, their large black coats like ravens wings fluttered in the wind, obscuring our view.

Ned stood between us, a hand on each of our shoulders, praying for my sister, praying for us.

Chapter 2

Through the weeks that followed I watched my mother change, until she became the empty shell that now dwelled within the confines of the house. She would sit at our table staring at the wall while I worked around her. First taking care of her and our home I would then turn my attention to our solitary source of income. I scraped by working as a costermonger, selling hot potatoes from our small wooden cart.

I remember ruefully how it had once been so easy. As my sister and I cooked my father sold, my mother making sure our clothes were fit for purpose, our rooms were clean and a hot meal was waiting for us at the end of a long day.

Then father left. The memory of his final farewell haunted me. Encompassing us in a wide embrace he had kissed our foreheads, before swinging his patched bag over his shoulder. Pressing his cap firmly upon his head he had walked through the door, his smile full of hope and promise.

With father gone mother was left to the cooking with Grace and me desperately trying to sell our produce. As the weeks rolled into months with no word from our father the cracks began to show. Slowly our room fell into disrepute and our clothes went unwashed as our mother slipped away from us. Grace and I would struggle up the street with the overladen cart before fighting to be heard over the din of the other traders.

I remember one day, our cart was pushed over by another costermonger as they walked past, our potatoes spilling over the dirty street. As I cried my sister had grabbed the side of the cart and hauled it back, the remaining few potatoes rolling noisily as it was dragged upright. With more exuberance than ever before my sister had carried on that day. She never stopped and she never complained, pushing the cart through the streets until her hands were blistered and her feet were raw from the miles she walked.

Then Grace got sick. It started with the headaches. I would watch as she raised her hand to her head, her eyes screwed tight against the light. Her appetite waned until eventually she stopped eating. I remember mother weeping, her hand clutching Graces shirt as she lay shivering, covered in a layer of sweat. That was when it was left to me to earn enough to support us.

Now, with Grace's death haunting my mother we were drifting through life, doing just enough to survive.

For breakfast I would place a hot potato on the table in front of mother before I left for work. Collecting my shawl I would show all pretences of leaving. Waiting a few moments I would then creep back into the house to watch her, observing her from the door with only one eye visible.

Today it seemed would be no different from the past few weeks. I watched, my hands clutching the door frame to prevent me from rushing to her side, as her eyes drifted to the food. She looked at it quizzically, like she did not know how it came to be there. My mother then lifted her hands and began picking at it piece by miniscule piece. As she pulled it apart her movements became more intense and erratic, her face distorting in a ghastly grimace. My knuckles would turn white as I gripped the door frame, ripped apart by my mother's sorrow. Tears would stream over her cheeks, her breath catching in her throat. She would inhale gulps of air as she lost control of her grief. Weeping she would destroy her food, the sobbing eventually subsiding as she went back to staring at the wall.

The day was just breaking as I pushed my cart onto the street. By starting early I hoped I could catch some early workers and get a head start on my competition. I would smile at the men as they walked past, trying to catch their eye. Fluttering my lashes I would stand like the prostitutes, one leg cocked at the knee, my hand resting lazily on my tattered skirt, the other twirling a lock of dirty blond hair in my fingers. I knew I was giving people the wrong idea but it brought the punters in.

I saw John across the street. He was new to Devils Acre, working on the ships that would dock nearby. He always made time to come and see me. I smiled as he sauntered over, his hands deep in his pockets, a knowing look in his eye. With my mother no longer talking to me and the loss of my sister still rife in my mind the attention I had from John mollified me.

As he came up to me he winked, asking in his strange accent, "so, how are the potatoes this morning?" I noticed he had the same role to his R's as Ned, although maybe his was more pronounced.

I giggled and dropped my gaze, unable to keep eye contact. He was lean and tanned, with defined muscles on his arms and torso. He wore a shirt buttoned to his navel, the rest hanging open, revealing his toned chest and a smattering of copper hair. His blond hair was tousled, falling casually into his light blue eyes. It was while I was marvelling him that I realised he was still waiting for a reply.

"I, well, umm, yes. They're lovely," I flashed him a brilliant smile before bravely adding, "As lovely as me."

He looked surprised by my remark and gave me a mischievous grin. It was the first time I had made a comment of this sort. I felt buoyed by his reaction; my wayward remark had caught him off guard.

"How's your sister, haven't seen her around for a while?" he asked, his head tilted to one side, a small smile playing across his lips.

"She, she was sick," I fumbled for the words, picking at the dry skin on the back of my hands.

"Is she better?" he asked, studying my face with his sharp blue eyes, he missed nothing.

"No, no she didn't get no better." I swallowed as I looked at my hands. I had torn a nail. It was hanging, broken and ragged by the smallest measure to the nail bed. I gripped it between my calloused fingers and tugged it hard. I felt a bite of pain as it was ripped away from the rest of the nail, a small spot of blood oozing from the nail bed. I wiped the crimson drop away on my dirtied skirt. "She's dead," I finished, finally meeting his gaze.

"That must be truly terrible for you and your family." He paused. "Tell me, how does it feel?"

"Excuse me?"

"How does it feel? I want to know how much it hurts," he said, his voice a low, growling whisper, his eyes wide and bright with excitement. He leaned in close, his nose nuzzling my hair as he breathed his next words into my ear. "I want to see your pain."

I stumbled away from him.

"What? I, I…" My voice broke as I stammered the words past my catching breaths. Trying to gain my footing I staggered back.

John followed me step for step until I was pinned to the side of my cart.

He pressed his body against mine, his hair tickling my cheek as his lips ran the length of my face. I could feel him breathing on my neck, his lips nearly touching mine. "Why don't we stop all this and I give you what we both know you want?"

I leaned away, scared by his bitter growl and the predatory look in his eyes. I tried to gather myself, to pull myself away from him but before I had time to think he grabbed the top of my arm, his fingers pinching into my soft flesh. I tried to jerk out of his grasp but his iron grip was too strong. He began marching me to the side of the street, leaving my cart and its produce to the fancies of the public.

"Let go of me! Ah, let go!" I raised my voice, hoping that someone would come to my aid. "Get off me! Let go!"

I thrashed against him; every time I pulled away he tightened his grip, yanking me off balance, the tops of my toes scraping the cobbles as I fell. He was forced to take all of my weight as my knee hit the floor. He dragged me to my feet with a rough shake and growled in my ear, "stand up and walk, or trust me, it'll be a lot worse for you."

I tried to bite his hand, my teeth grazing his knuckles, when his other hand sealed over my mouth, clenching my jaw firmly shut.

No one came to my aid.

I stamped on his feet, digging my heel into his foot as he dragged me deeper into the obscurities of the alley. When the street was no more than a bright spot of activity in the distance he threw me to the ground, my head hitting the street floor. My vision swam; when I focused, my view was taken up by John standing over me, a malicious grin smeared across his handsome face.

"Well now, someone's been a naughty girl. Do you know what happens to naughty girls?"

"Please, I didn't mean anything by it. I was just copying what the girls do on the corner. I…I don't want this. Please, just let me go." Tears were flooding down my face. I scrambled back on my heels and palms until my back hit the wall.

"You are pathetic, aren't you? Say it! Say, I am pathetic."

I looked up at him in disgust; I had no choice but to indulge his sick fantasy. "I am pathetic," I repeated in a small voice, barely above a whisper.

He laughed cruelly, gazing down upon his prey. His head swayed from side to side, his hands deep in his pockets once more. The dirty smirk never once left his face.

"Good. Now, take off your clothes."

"W…wh…what?"

He leant over and whispered silkily, "what? What? Are you stupid? I said, take off your clothes. Now."

I did not move.

"Do you want to end up like your sister?"

"What do you know about my sister?" I spluttered, frozen in a new type of fear.

"I know everything about your sister. I had plans for her, just like I have plans for you." He smiled sickeningly, stepping back to admire his new toy, leaning back, assessing me keenly.

As John looked up the ally, checking for onlookers, I took my chance. I scrambled to my feet, with one hand pressed against the unforgiving wall I started to run. I made it three strides before John grabbed me around the waist, my cry cut short as the breath was squeezed from my lungs by his unrelenting arm.

"Where do you think you're going?" he growled, specks of spit hitting my cheek as he breathed heavily in my ear.

I thrashed against him, trying to free myself.

"Enough!" he shouted as he threw me to the floor.

He advanced on me like a rabid dog, ready, waiting, pining to rip me limb from limb. Cornered and out of options I pulled my legs inwards.

"Well, what should we be doing about all this?"

The voice came from my right. It was my knight in shining armour. Or rather, it was Ned; but I knew at that moment I was safe.

John looked smugly at Ned. As I stared I saw John's face change, a flicker of something behind his eyes, recognition or fear, I was not sure.

"You shouldn't be here," Ned stated quietly, dangerously. "You've done enough. Taken enough. Let it go."

John quickly regained his composure. "This is nothing to do with you old man. Just turn around, walk away." He had a dark smile, a smile full of threat.

Ned shot me a reassuring smile before turning his attention back to John.

"This has everything to do with me." As he spoke he casually leant against the side of the alley, throwing a quick glance behind him, "and I will not just turn around and, as you say, walk away. But rather beat you until you learn how a lady is to be treated." He could have been discussing the weather for all anyone listening behind closed doors knew. I however, had known Ned for many years and could see the carefully disguised anger burning behind his eyes.

John ignited first. "WHO IN HELL…"

Ned exploded with the power of a charging bull, tackling John at the waist and driving him to the floor. As they hit the ground Ned pounced on him, punching him over and over in a relentless violent attack. John, taken off guard, had no chance to defend himself.

Rather than rein Ned in, as I had at the brothel, I thought it best to let him continue his tirade. By the time he had finished John was no longer demure and dashing, but rather a pulped body that moved and breathed. He coughed, a globule of congealed blood and phlegm hanging from the side of his mouth. His eyes were drifting madly, his pupils dilated. I watched as blood crept across the white of one eye.

"I'll get you. I'll get you you bitch," he spat from the muck. "You wait. You'll never be safe; you'll never be alone," he growled, his pupils dilating as he lay on his back.

Ned kicked a clump of frozen dirt at his face, silencing his frenzied rant and pulled me to my feet. Brushing me off the best he could he gave me the first genuine smile I had seen all day. I tried to return the gesture but found I could not manage it. My eyes dropped to the floor, I felt ashamed of myself; the position I had put myself in and how I had pushed everyone's warnings to the side. I had been reckless.

"Thank you," I started to say in a small voice.

Ned cut me short, holding up a blood-smeared hand. "Don't even think about apologising. He's a nasty piece of work. It wasn't your fault; he had you pegged long ago." A troubled look flared across his face, his worry turning to fear as he saw my questioning frown. He forced a look of condescending concern onto his face. "But now that I come to think about it, it may not be a bad idea to stop copying the women on the corner. That may not have done you any favours, if you catch my drift?" he continued, giving me a knowing look. "Let's keep this little run-in to ourselves. I don't think your dear mother can cope with much more."

We walked back to my cart in silence, both lost in thought. My absence had not gone unnoticed. I had left with my cart half-full but it now stood, emptied of every crumb. Luckily John had not robbed me before trying to rape me so I had something to show for my work. Looking at my earnings it would be enough to cover the rent but nothing more.

It was still early and if I hurried I should have enough time to do a second run of potatoes, recovering some of the money I had lost. I thanked Ned again as I began collecting the scattered remains of my trade. He dipped an imaginary hat before making his way down the street. I collected my cart and wrapped my shawl over my shoulders, tucking it under my arms before heading home.

I needed to focus on my mother, her demons came from within. She had an unrelenting torture of the mind, where she had nowhere to hide. Neither thought nor memory would be left untainted by the pungent fears that infested her. I had seen many people consumed by the terrors of their past. Their world slowly disintegrating around them, with nothing left in life to cling to. They would stop functioning and slip away into nothingness, eventually dying of starvation, hypothermia or some neglectful illness. I could not allow this fate to befall my mother.

Before long I was rounding the last corner of my street, stepping over the trail of raw sewage. I gave the door a hard shove, the hinges creaking as it swung inwards. I made my way down the dark, dirty corridor to our room. As I stepped inside, something about the room seemed off, my senses picking up on aspects of the room my conscious mind was yet to catch up on. Nothing had changed or moved since I had left that morning, yet my mother was not in the chair at the table. I moved deeper into the house. It was dark and voiceless, all light kept at bay by a rag hung over the window; the only sound coming from rats scurrying over the bare floor.

I leant my head over the fire, checking the potatoes I had put to roast that morning. I was met with a burnt smell. Coughing, I covered my mouth with the corner of my shirt as I took a closer look. The potatoes sat in the position I had left them, charred to the roasting plate.

I looked up and studied the room, not even the dust had been disturbed. A heavy atmosphere seemed to hang in the air, causing the hairs on my arm and the back of my neck to stand on end. I quietly stepped through the kitchen and crept around the corner to our bedroom. That is where I found my mother. She was huddled in the corner on our pile of rags. As she rocked I could hear her murmuring.

I stumbled towards her; the sounds of my bare feet scuffing the dirt seemed to rouse her from her trance. I looked into her dull eyes but they showed no recognition. She lost her focus as the muttering continued.

"Mother, mother, a…are you, feeling well? Mother?"

She did not reply. I scrambled up to her, leaning my ear close to her mouth.

"He's coming, he's coming, he's coming…" was all she would whisper between short, sharp, agonised gasps. "He's coming, he's coming, he's coming…"

Her fingers gripped her knees with such ferocity, her knuckles white, the skin stretched so thin I thought it would split. Her fingernails had been bitten and picked until they bled, the dry blood streaked down her face where she had wiped away endless tears. I grabbed her arm, shaking her, desperately trying to rouse a response. "Who's coming, who do you think is coming mother?"

"YOU HAVE TO RUN!" she suddenly screamed in a heart-wrenchingly desperate voice as she leaned forward, her thin fingers pulling at my shirt.

Her breathing intensified as the panic engulfed her, her eyes wide with fear.

After a few panicked breaths her eyes glazed over as she reverted to staring at the wall, her lank hair falling into her lifeless eyes; the unrelenting muttering continuing.

"Come now mother, no one is coming. Where are we going to run?" I sat back, waiting for her to say something, when no response was given I tried again. "Do you fancy helping me with the potatoes? Let's get you out of this house; some fresh morning air would do you good."

All of my attempts fell short of forming a reaction, any reaction. Wanting with all my heart to stay and warm her cold frame, I knew if I did not work we would not live.

I took off my shawl and wrapped it over my mother's shoulders. "I'll be back soon," I whispered, "I promise." I pressed my lips to her dirty hair, inhaling the dank smell of unwashed skin, before leaving.

With a weighted chest I reloaded my cart with the burnt potatoes, making my way back to my selling point. I sold what I could but was not as focussed as I should have been, my mind constantly falling back to my mother. It was a fruitless endeavour. Every time I closed my eyes a different nightmare was waiting for me. Grace withering on the bed, slowly slipping away; John standing over me, a cruel grin stretched across his evil face; my mother rocking on the floor, a fragment of whom she had once been.

With each blazing memory burning in my mind I felt a jolt of fear course through my body. I looked down to see my hands shaking, my whole body beginning to quake. I leant against the side of the cart, rubbing my face with my hands. I needed to stay my fretful mind and quiet my restless heart. I had made very little money and half the potatoes were ruined.

As the afternoon slowly rolled into evening the sun began sinking behind the tall building. With heavy feet and trembling hands I collected my cart and started making my way home. As I stumbled down the street I saw a group of urchins running towards me. They were barrelling down the road. Before I had a chance to move they were upon me. The first boy rushed past, causing me to spin to the right. Another tore past, clipping my shoulder, pushing me to the left. I stumbled, only just catching myself, as three more hurtled past. I was jarred and jolted as each boy crashed past me. As they knocked into me I was twirled on the spot until I saw the floor coming up to meet me. I landed in a heap on the road.

As they disappeared around the far corner I brushed off my hands. I took my time, examining the ingrained dirt that had collected in the little groves of my fingers from my years of hard labour. I worked my way over my body, checking for any damage. As I was pushing the hair from of my eyes I saw fresh blood on my hand. Putting my hand to my brow I found the fine trickle tracking down to my eyebrow. I wiped it off, applying pressure with a corner of my ragged shirt.

It was as I was checking a graze on my knee that I noticed the familiar pull of my secret pocket, full of the day's earnings, was no longer there. I had no idea which one had done the deed but they had robbed me of every half penny I had. They must have been scouting me all day, waiting until the end, planning their attack carefully. I had nothing else worth selling, no food fit for the table and no money for rent. I had no choice, no option left to me, I would have to go home and beg the landlord to let us stay on the promise that I repay the debt.

The last glimmers of a decaying sun fell upon a rose stained sky as I battled through the bustling streets. At this time of night it was hectic, full of people wanting to get home or wanting to get to the closest pub or brothel. I was jostled from side to side as I dragged my cart towards home. With the crowd finally thinning I took the final few streets at a jog.

A dark blanket was falling over Devils Acre. The tall buildings shutting out the moonlight and the industrial smoke obscuring all but the brightest of stars made me feel oppressed. The crushing realities of my life being pressed upon me by the suffocating film of night.

I stumbled through the darkness, guided alone by the repetition of walking down this road for a lifetime. I negotiated the brothel carefully, skipping past the front door as a customer relieved himself on the front step. I hurried on, missing the shawl I had given my mother earlier that day.

Through the darkness I could see a crowd surrounding our front door. I could see men stood at the back, craning their necks to get a better look. Children trying to shoulder their way to the front, wriggling from their mothers grasp. Women stood further back, clutching their shawls and coats, muttering behind their hands as they cast wary glances to the crowd. They had no reason to be there. All the scenarios that could cause this level of commotion ran through my mind as I approached. My breath caught in my throat as realization dawned.

Mother.

Anxiety ripped through me as adrenalin coursed through my veins. I dropped the cart and broke into a run. My breaths came in gasps as my heart raced; pain leaching from every surface of my body. A crescendo of drums beat upon my chest. As I reached the horde of mismatched bodies I bowed and lunged, pushing my bare feet harder into the cobbles, desperately fighting against the sea of people.

I did not care what people thought of me, did not care who I was kicking, barging past. I heard shouts of indignation and concern as I pushed further on through the melee. An unknown arm wrapped around my shoulders. I was too fixated on my mother's fate to see who was there. I bit into the arm and heard a yelp as the arm retracted. Finally I burst over the threshold.

She was still hanging from the beam she had used to end her life, surrendering her soul to what lay beyond.

Chapter 3

The chair she had climbed on and kicked away still lay on its side on the floor, her body framed by the peeling walls of the hallway. My eyes came level with her dangling feet as I fell to my knees. I could feel myself shaking, could hear a woman screaming in the background that cut above all other sound. I kept telling myself that the images before me were not real. They could not be real.

People crowded around me, their faces, expressions, lost in time as my world stopped. My life suspended, my eyes drawn to her hanging legs that swung like a pendulum to the pull of my painful breaths. Suddenly, crushingly, the world caught up with me; the noise of the crowd swamping my deluged senses. Some men were trying to take charge of the situation; I heard one calling for a sharp knife, another for a sheet to wrap her in. I heard a man asking for me to be removed from the house, telling people I should not be here. Others were not so kind. There was a group ransacking our room, our rags being picked through. Anything of value or use was being taken. Despite all the voices, all the uproar, all I could see were her dirty feet, blue and swollen from where the blood had pooled in her extremities.

I felt hands grasping my shoulders, pulling me to my feet. Grabbing my arms they propelled me back; the men making an impenetrable wall before me. I was trapped with no way out of my nightmare. I fell to my knees as grief flaunted itself upon my body. As I crawled over the filthy ground towards my mother I could see glimpses through the crowd's legs, like cracks in old floor boards. They were preparing to cut her down. A man was bending, picking up the chair that had been my mother's last foothold on life. I could almost feel her last moments, the despair of having no way out of our squalid existence; of knowing that there was nothing left for her here. The bitter thought stabbed a hot spear of resentment through my lost heart, spoiling the already squandered memories of my mother.

An arm came out of nowhere, wrapping itself firmly around my waist. I was hoisted into the air, kicking and struggling against the unyielding grip. In one swift move I was thrown over my captor's shoulder. My hysterical screams alerted no one to my cause. I was nothing but a lost child to them, no one could help me now. The man was carrying me away, away from a house that was no longer my home. Looking up I saw a last image of my mother, her body being cradled to the floor by her closest friends as the rope was cut.

The man who held me hostage did not utter a word as he made off with me down the street. I had given up. Whatever my fate, I had nothing left here but nightmares and lost memories.

I was still sobbing, my strength spent, when I heard footsteps behind us. A shiver of fear ran through my body. All memory of this morning had abandoned me until this moment. It was not until then that I remembered my confrontation with John. For all I knew this man could be taking me to him now. I began struggling, trying to free myself once more. No matter what I did he would not let go, he merely quickened his pace.

The stranger had carried me through the slums, eventually coming out at a back alley I did not recognise. A cloud shifted, revealing a bright crescent moon; in its light I recognised the incredible structure of Westminster Abbey looming in front of us. Here is where he came to rest; pulling me from his shoulder he placed me gently on my feet.

I looked up, surprised to see Adam Brewer standing before me. His light-brown eyes showed nothing but sadness, his delicately featured face worn and full of remorse. He knelt down and looked into my eyes. "I'm so sorry. We were taking it in turns to watch her. It was my watch tonight but Lizzie was sick. Everyone knew how ill your mother was. You can't go back there, it's too dangerous." Throughout this redundant explanation his eyes kept wandering the street, staring into the bleak night.

I did not understand what he meant by dangerous but had no energy to question his motives. Somewhere, buried deep behind the pain of losing my mother, I felt the soft warmth of love. They had tried to help. They had been looking after my mother and me after all. I could not manage a reply. I just looked at him, desperate for answers, for help.

I was suddenly distracted, the footsteps had returned. My head followed Adams as he stared into the street. Someone was coming. Whoever they were, they were keeping to the shadows, keeping out of sight. They were catching up to us, the footfalls now falling in a faster repetition. I scooted behind Adam and peaked from behind his jacket.

A large cloaked figure stepped out from the shadows; I saw the head swing towards the quiet street, checking for onlookers, before pulling back the hood. It was Ned, his breathing heavy as he looked to Adam. "Nobody followed us, we got away clean." His eyes swept the street once more. "Anywhere to stay tonight?" he asked.

"Sorry Ned, couldn't find anywhere. We could go straight there? They would have to let us in eventually."

At last Ned turned to me, a bleak expression on his face. "I wish there was something I could say." He looked distraught, reaching out a hand he laid it on my shoulder. "You have got to understand Clara; there was nothing you could have done to prevent what happened to her. I know what you're feeling but you can't go back, you can never go back."

"Why? Please Ned. I just want to go home," I begged, trying to shrug away from him.

"No Clara," Ned said more forcibly. "Let's find somewhere warm for tonight." He took me by the hand and started leading me further away from my old home. As we walked he looked behind and called back to Adam. "Thanks Brewer. I'll give you a rundown of events tomorrow."

I pulled away from him, fully intending to run back with Adam but Ned would not allow it.

"No Clara, it's not safe."

"Why…"

Ned cut me off, "I can't tell you why, not here, not now. I just need to make sure you are safe. You can never go back to Devils Acre; you can never come back here, he'll find you."

"Who will find me?"

"John. You can never let him find you."

Ned's eyes swung the length of the street. "I've got to get you somewhere safe. This way." He turned and marched me down the street, stopping at every crossroad, every alley, to check we were not being followed.

As we reached a corner I turned, expecting to see Adam still watching us, or a ghostly figure creeping amongst the misshapen shops. Terrified, I looked behind, only to find an empty street.

I trailed behind Ned, my thoughts on my painful loss. The emptiness inside was all-consuming, the fear feeding it, giving it an edge of fire as it ripped my body apart. The more I tried to process what had happened the more chaotic my mind became. My head started to ache, I felt like I was walking through thick fog. As I inhaled the air burnt my throat. I was struggling to walk, dragging the air into my lungs when I fell to my knees, my palms hitting the unforgiving street. I started retching, my world spinning out of control as the street became hazy. Suddenly the ground disappeared beneath me and I felt myself floating; my world finally going dark.

Someone was screaming, the high pitch searing through my head. I ran backwards, trying to get away from the blinding sound. Suddenly I was falling, falling as earth rose on either side of me. Looking up I could see ravens circling high above, calling to death itself, while limbs of a dead tree clawed through a steel grey sky like some forgotten foe. I turned and Graces body was next to me, her eyes staring blankly ahead.

"Is she alright? Looks a little peaky?" The female's voice invaded my thoughts.

I was sure I had seen my sister's blue decaying lips move in time to the words.

"You would too after what she's been through." Ned's voice swam to me from the darkness.

Ned was stood above me, looking into the grave. With a sad shake of his head he swung a rope over a large branch of the tree. Pulling the rope tight, my mother's corpse was hoisted into the air before being slowly lowered into the grave.

"Nasty business, that's for sure. What are you going to do?" someone said, a man's voice, a gentle voice.

'Help me, you need to help me!' I screamed as earth was shovelled onto us. I could feel the earth hitting my face. No, it was beads of water; I could feel the small drops running down the sides of my forehead.

"You can stay here for tonight and we'll decide what to do then." This time it was a woman who spoke.

The voices swimming in and out of my head began to come into focus. I was lying on something soft. Something cool was being wiped across my forehead. I raised my hand, trying to brush away the mystery object.

"Now now. You just lie still like a good girl."

The hand was being persistent. I could not form the words to make it stop. I shook my head, a moan escaping my lips. My eyes flickered open, focussing on a bright spot that was swaying above me. Realization quickly dawned. I had no family, no home and had no idea where I was. I struggled to sit-up, pushing away the hands trying to restrain me. My breathing became faster, more erratic; I had no way of controlling the panic that had overtaken my body.

The voices were rising around me, calling to me like disembodied fiends, calling me to my nightmares. I was spinning, trying to find a hold on the moment. My world was spiralling out of control and I was falling with it.

Ned swam into view above me. He gripped my shoulders and shook me to my senses.

"Clara. Hey. Clara. It's me, Ned. Can you see me? Clara!"

I could see him looking deep into my eyes. The more I studied him the more in focus he became. Everything shifted, becoming more tangible, as my eyes worked their way around the room.

Behind Ned stood a woman with a heart-shaped face; her soft eyes crinkled at the corners as she surveyed me, her brow creased in concern. My eyes numbly worked their way over her body. A dark blue dress covered her vast bosom over which she wore a starched white apron with a pocket sewn onto the front, a clean rag and set of keys hanging precariously from it. My eyes tracked down her pinafore to her feet where she was wearing black lace-up boots with a small heel. There was detailing on the toe of the boots, a pretty swirling pattern that wound its way around the base. My eyes drifted back up over her body until I was met with her caring gaze once more.

She smiled and bent down. "Let me guess, you're famished? On your feet now, let's get you some soup."

Ned held out his hands and helped me to my feet. He nestled me under his arm as he walked me through the house. There were numerous oil lamps hanging from the ceiling or perched precariously on sideboards, giving the house a bright warm glow. On every available space there were shoes of every shape and size and in varying levels of completion. There were pieces of leather, reams of shoe laces and new and tarnished buckles, all hanging on nails tacked to the walls.

As I stumbled through the house the bare floorboards creaked, causing muted light to glimmer through the gaps. I could hear a gentle tapping coming from below, the grind of a chair and the noise of heavy-booted feet. I realized we were above a shop. Her husband must be a cobbler, living above where they made their livelihood. We passed through a small archway to her kitchenette.

There was a small stove in the corner on which sat a pan, its contents bubbling away, wafting its inviting aromas towards me. The woman led me to her table, sat me down on a chair and gestured for Ned to sit opposite. She bustled around us, collecting plates, bowls and cutlery. She reached onto a shelf above the stove and took down a loaf of bread that had been hidden under a piece of cloth.

Within minutes we had thick doorsteps of bread piled high on our plates and a bowl of hot broth sat in front of us. It was at that moment I realised I had not eaten properly in days, weeks. I tore off a piece of bread, dunked it into the broth and felt warmed through as I placed it in my mouth. I savoured every mouthful of the elixir, trying to commit the taste to memory. I finished by eagerly gulping down the cup of water she had placed in front of me. I wiped my mouth on the back of my arm.

"Would you like some more?" she asked, obviously amused rather than offended by my poor table manners.

"It was lovely, thank you, but I think I've eaten enough." I smiled sheepishly at her as she nodded and turned her attention to the stove. I looked across at Ned, who was on his third portion; he managed to give me a cheeky grin through his mouthful of food. At that moment I was eternally grateful to him. Through all of his turmoil and heartache he had always been looking out for me.

"You can sleep here tonight, the girl can have the sofa and you're more than welcome to the floor," the woman stated from the corner.

Looking out of the small kitchen window I saw nothing but darkness, the streets silent at this late hour. Ned saw me looking and immediately stood, walking over to the window he pulled the curtains closed before gesturing for me to stand. As I traipsed back through to the sofa, his comforting hand on my shoulder, I saw him exchange a meaningful glance with the woman. Too consumed with my own ordeal to give it much thought I fell onto the cushions. I felt a blanket being draped over my body. Trying desperately to fight the fatigue consuming my body I felt my eyes beginning to close. Despite my defiant mind I was asleep in minutes. The nightmares thankfully kept at bay by my exhaustion.

I awoke the next morning to the sound of raised voices from below. I lay still, my eyes shut, listening to the conversation.

"I'm telling you, it's not my fault."

"So what happened, the shoe pixie came along and broke them?"

"No. I'm saying you should not have worn them when you went for that little paddle in the Thames a few months ago."

"What are you accusing me of exactly?"

"I saw you! You got drunk and took that unexpected trip into the Thames. I'm guessing you didn't clean them and that's why they're now falling apart at the seams. They're fixable, but it'll cost you, and I want the money up front."

"The money up front?" the man spluttered. "To hell with that! You've not heard the last of this!"

I heard footsteps, the tinkle of a bell and the door slamming shut. A man sighed heavily as he muttered under his breath. The house fell quiet once more.

With nothing left to distract me, I could no longer pretend to be in my deep slumber. I opened my eyes and pushed myself up to sitting, the blanket falling to the floor. It was as I was stretching and rubbing the sleep from my eyes that I realized Ned was nowhere to be seen. I picked up the blanket, placing it on the sofa in my absence and gingerly made my way through the house. It was as I remembered it from the night before, only the lamps had been extinguished and the curtains pulled back.

The view through the window finally revealed where we were. I was looking down into one of the market streets of London. It was a bustle of activity, the shops beginning to open for their day's trade. There were young boys cleaning the shop fronts, girls sweeping the paths and men laying out their displays for the public. The scene was overlooked by a weak sun sat low in the sky, pushing its diminished rays of light through the heavy cloud cover.

I made my way through to the kitchen where I found Ned and the mystery woman sat talking in low voices. As I approached I heard her say, "if there was any more I could do, I would. I've spoken to George and he agrees that we just can't afford it."

Ned looked disappointed but as I came closer he forced a smile onto his face. "I've got to go out for a while. Betty here will sort you out for breakfast. I'll be back before lunch." With that he got up and left without so much as a ba ckward glance.

Looking over my shoulder at Ned's retreating back I walked to the table, tentatively sitting on a chair.

"Sleep well Clara? I would have thought so, you looked exhausted," she twittered, as she set a plate of buttered bread in front of me, "butter, fresh this morning, got out early especially to get it."

As I ate I tried to think of what was going to happen to me next. It was obvious from the conversation I had just overheard that I couldn't stay here, but where to go and how to get money to live was an idea that was beyond my grasp.

"Fresh butter is lovely, isn't it? A nice little treat for you." Betty was still talking at me.

I nodded, smiled and agreed in all the right places, while inside my world was falling apart. I was grasping at the things that had made up my life; my family, my friends, my home. They were like grains of sand I was trying to hold in my hands. The harder I held the faster they were slipping away.

As the morning progressed I had nothing to do except sit and watch the clock make its tentative way towards eleven o'clock. Betty had gone to help her husband in the shop leaving me to my own devices. I sat alone, scared and isolated.

At five past eleven I heard the shop door open. I could hear muffled voices, spoken too low for me to make out. There was silence and then the sound of footsteps coming up the stairs. I waited with bated breath to see if Ned had returned. A moment later he swung round the corner with Betty following in his wake.

"Betty and George have agreed for you to stay here, just for now, until I can get something else sorted out. Don't leave the shop, stay inside, keep yourself safe and keep out of trouble." Ned then looked to Betty. "Thank you. I'll come by every week. She's a good worker."

"What's going on Ned?" I asked, desperate for answers.

"Not enough hours in the day to say," Ned answered, refusing to meet my eye. "I'd best be off. Betty, I thank you and George again, I must be off. Clara, I'll see you very soon. Be good."

I saw he was about to leave. Running up to him I flung my arms round his vast chest and wept, the tears spilling freely from my burning eyes. He pushed me gently away and leaned down to talk to me, his face now level with mine. "Don't be afraid, you'll be safe here and you'll be seeing me again before you know it," he said, wiping my tears away with his rough skinned thumbs. With that he stood, dipped his cap and walked away.

The days soon fell into weeks as I awaited Ned's return. Betty and George did well to keep me occupied and I soon found myself immersed in the running of the shop. George patiently showed me how to polish shoes and thread laces and by the end of the second week I was to be found sat on a high stall behind the counter, polishing the shoes before they went back to their owners.

I was resting on the sofa, full from Betty's soup and tired from helping George, when I heard the bell tinkle from below as the door to the shop was opened.

"Is she asleep?" I heard a man whisper.

"She's resting, yes," I heard Betty reply.

"This is all I could get. I know it's not as much as we agreed, but it's all I've got." I recognised the voice, the accent. It was Ned.

I rolled up to sitting, causing my makeshift bed to groan ominously, but froze as I caught the next sentence.

"Is he still out there, is he still looking for her?" Betty asked in an urgent whisper.

"Yes, it looks like he's gone underground. He knows I've hidden her but he doesn't know where."

"She can stay a bit longer, but Ned, we need more than this."

"I know. I'll sort something out."

I heard heavy footsteps make their way to the door.

"Should we tell her you came by?" I heard Betty's voice call the length of the shop.

"No, don't tell her anything, not yet. Just keep her safe."

"We will."

With that the bell chimed and the door closed with a snap. A long silence followed, with only the shifting of shoes below to break it.

"We can't keep her love," I heard George mutter.

"Just give him a little more time. Give him a chance to sort something out. She can't go to the workhouse." Betty's voice broke on the last word. "You know what it's like, what they're like. You saw that report in the paper. The men in there; they found them starving, sucking the marrow from the rotting bones they were made to sort through."

"Hush now, hush," George soothed. "That won't happen to Clara. Remember what else they said. They said they were making it better; giving them proper food, making it a better place. The children even have schooling now."

I lay back on the bed. I had heard the stories of the workhouse, all the slum kids had. They would beat you to the point of death, starve you until you begged for water and work you until your hands bled. The very mention of the place made my heart constrict with raw fear.

Weeks rolled by with no sign of Ned. I could see how much strain I was putting Betty and George under. Their whispered rows did not go unheard; the reduction in our food did not go unseen.

Then, one day, it happened.

I was upstairs, replacing a pair of shoelaces, when I heard the bell ding from the shops counter. It struck me then that I had not heard the bell tinkle that hung above the shops door. They must have come through the back. I clambered off the horsehair stuffed sofa and went to walk down stairs as voices floated through the floorboards. Suddenly I froze, it was Ned. Crouched at the top of the stairs, I listened.

"I know, I know," he was saying, "it's all sorted. I've been there this morning, she has an appointment and we can't be late." I heard a murmur and the grinding of a chair before, "no, don't, I'll get her."

I stared, sat on the top step, my hands gripping the wooden uprights of the rail as he walked slowly up the stairs.

"Where are we going?" I asked, as a spike of fear fired through my body.

He would not answer; he just held out his hand and waited for me to take it. He steered me down the stairs. At the bottom I came face to face with George. I noticed how creased and worn his shirt was as it hung off his tall, lanky frame. His black hair swept over to one side, poorly disguising the bald patch atop his head. He rubbed my cheek with his thumb, his fingers under my chin keeping my face looking towards him. He studied me for a brief moment, worry etched on his face.

"Look after yourself kid." He turned to Ned. "Sorry we couldn't help more."

As we made our way through the vast piles of shoes and repairs I saw Betty waiting for us by the door. She had tears rolling down her cheeks, a handkerchief clutched to her chest, no longer bothering to wipe the salty streaks away. As I came up to her she pulled me into a bracing hug. "You be a good girl and do what they say and you'll be alright," she whispered as she caressed my cheek, kissed my head. I wove my fingers into the fabric of her dress and pulled myself close to her. She stood and held me until Ned cleared his throat. I felt her pull away, her hands on my shoulders. I clung to her, unwilling to let go. Slowly I freed the folds of her dress from my yearning fingers and she released me, touching my hair, my shoulder, placing her hand over my heart before stepping back.

Ned held the door open for me and with one last look at Betty, George and the shop I stepped outside. Ned followed me out, closing the door behind me. Together we walked through the unfamiliar streets.

"They said to be there for twelve o' clock. Don't want to be late. Keep up Clara, it's quite a walk."

Ned dragged me on through the teeming streets by my hand. My fingers lost in his large fist. I kept slightly behind him, in his wake I was protected from the crowds. I stayed close, my other hand clutching the hem of his coat.

After what felt like an age we rounded another corner and came out at yet another busy street. I looked up at Ned, pulling on his coat to get his attention, to ask him how much further it was when my words were lost, lost to his dark gaze. I followed his eyes to the end of the street and came to an abrupt halt. The workhouse loomed ahead, the unforgiving stone structure dominating all neighbouring buildings. He took me by the arm as I started backing away and carried on walking.

"Ned, what are you doing? I can't go in there! Ned stop!"

He stopped walking and turned to me, the pain now obvious on his face. "I'm sorry. I never wanted this. There's nowhere else for you to go. I've tried to find you work and lodgings, but there is no one who can help. It'll be okay. Just keep your head down and do your work. You will have food and a place to sleep while you're there. It's the best I can do for you now."

I looked slowly from the workhouse to Ned; despite my fear I could see no option but to follow him. As we neared the gates my heart rate increased, pounding, beating and battering my chest, my breath hitching, catching in my throat. In my head I was screaming at myself to turn, to run, that anything would be better than this.

As we made our final approach my eyes stung, my throat becoming clogged with my desire to run. A massive archway marked the entrance to the workhouse, a high exterior wall enclosing the compound. On the other side of the arch was a set of broad iron gates. A marshal was stood waiting for me impatiently on the other side, his dark, impassive gaze coldly considering me. Ned released me as tears spilled down my cheeks, falling one after another to the floor, each tear a drop of hope leaving my soul. I took a deep breath and gathered all my courage as I took my first steps towards captivity. I now understood why this was known as 'The Archway of Tears.'

Chapter 4

I walked up to the gate, tears streaming from my eyes. The marshal turned to me, looking at me down his long thin nose, a pair of round glasses magnifying his watery blue eyes. His weak chin puckered as he pinched his lip between plaque encrusted teeth, assessing me.

"Name?" he eventually barked.

"Clara."

"Clara, what?"

"Elizabeth Forge. Clara Elizabeth Forge," I stuttered.

"Date of Birth?"

"July 21st 1872."

"And that would make you?"

"T…t…twelve?" I answered.

"You're expected. Follow me."

I looked up at him in surprise. Is this what Ned had been organising? The marshal opened the gate and escorted me inside. I jumped as they slammed behind me. I could see Ned watching me fixedly outside the gates. There was no more he could do for me now. I turned my back on my last remaining friend and walked.

I was in a large plain court yard. There was neither a tree nor blade of grass to break up the monotonous brick. The building was bigger than I had first thought. There were five large windows to either side of a grand front door, the building itself standing three stories high. The doors and windows were closed; staring intently I could see no flicker of movement or signs of life from behind the dark panes.

I had expected to head towards the front doors but instead was lead around the side of the building and up a flight of narrow brick steps that made their way to the middle floor. From this angle I could see more of the same faceless buildings behind. As I came to the top of the steps I was confronted by a small wooden door. The marshal removed a large set of keys from his jacket pocket. As the key was turned the door swung open with a loud echoing groan. I found myself in a cold corridor that was no more comforting than outside.

"Stand here, wait for my return," he said looking up the corridor before continuing to drawl at me, "this is the infirmary. You never know, you might just find yourself in here on a more permanent basis," he sneered, leaning in close, his putrid breath coating the inside of my mouth.

He tilted back, assessing me once more, before turning and marching up the corridor, malevolently banging adjoining doors as he went, spreading fear down the corridor like a plague. I heard a woman scream as he banged on her door, begging him to stop.

He paused, backtracking to where the woman had shrieked. He looked at me down the corridor before placing a finger over his lips, a smile playing across his mouth. He barged through the door, bursting into the room. Despite not being able to see, I had no allusions of what was happening inside. I could hear her weeping, crying for him to get off, pleading with him to stop.

Eventually he sauntered out of the room, lazily walking towards me as he readjusted his shirt and trousers. As he came level with me he wiped a trail of blood from the corner of his mouth.

"Not long 'til the bitch'll be dead anyway," he smirked.

I stared at the wall in front of me, not daring to look up or move. Out of the corner of my eye I watched him admire the blood on his finger before smearing it across my cheek.

"And that's my promise to you," he whispered in my ear. "Wait here, not a foot moves," he clipped loudly, his voice reverberating off the walls, before once more strolling up the corridor.

It was not long before the marshal was marching back through the echoing hallway.

"The meeting has already concluded; you will have to wait until tomorrow. This way."

He took me by the shoulder and shoved me outside, forcing me to run down the steps ahead of him. He strode past me, leaving me to catch my breath as I tried to follow. Coming back around to the front of the building he knocked on the front door and after a few minutes an elderly lady answered.

"Do you have space for one more?" he asked. For the first time I heard him use a respectful tone when speaking to someone.

"I will find her a place for the night," she answered in an authoritative tone.

"In," she ordered bluntly, gesturing with her thumb for me to go inside.

I found myself in a large foyer with three long corridors stretching before me, one left, one right and one dead ahead. Large windows stood at the far end of each passage allowing the atrium to be flooded with light. The old woman strode purposely down the hallway ahead, leaving me to stumble in her wake. Looking up I could see oil lamps hung by fine chains along the long stretch of passage. As we walked I saw some of the doors stood open. I peeked inside. Lying on the beds were both old and young in varying degrees of sickness. Some writhed in agony while others stared blankly, like hollow shells, their souls already lost to the shadows.

We reached the end room where she stopped to unlock a door. She pushed it open, revealing a mass of people, all in rags. Some stood alone with no one to cling to, others in family groups, huddled together for comfort and warmth. Stepping inside, I wandered into the crowd. I heard the door lock behind me with a terrifying finality. As I walked amongst the people I noticed piles of straw stacked on the floor, in the middle of the room stood a bucket that, I could see by its contents, was to be our toilet.

I made my way to the corner of the room, gathering some straw into my own personal hoard before huddling on the floor. I sat and studied people for what felt like hours. I watched as a mother sat humming to her child, rocking her gently. The mother had her eyes closed, as if committing every moment, every note, to memory. As she finished humming her song she bent her head, inhaling the smell of her daughter's hair.

As day moved into night I heard a commotion by the door. A group of servant girls came in carrying large baskets. They were surrounded immediately by a group vying for first pick of the food. As the commotion calmed the girls moved through the room, handing out hunks of bread and blocks of cheese and ladling water into small cups from which people feverishly drank. These were our rations for the night. I hid my stash of the food under my shirt and nibbled at it, determined to make it last. As I lifted a small piece of cheese to my lips a man gripped my hand, twisting it painfully until my morsel of food fell to the floor. The crumb was quickly snatched by a small child who ran into the crowd, leaving the man empty handed.

"What else you got?" he snarled, twisting my wrist harder still.

"No, nothing, I have nothing more," I cried, my face screwed up in pain.

"You're lying," he growled, dragging me from my bed of straw.

My legs uncurled as I was pulled across the urine soaked floor, the bread and cheese becoming untangled from my shirt. As soon as the man saw it he stopped. He bent over me, grabbing what he could of the food before others started fighting for it. All I could do was roll into a ball and wait for the attack to stop. The wind was knocked from my lungs as someone's knee was forced against my chest and an unseen foot landed painfully on my leg. Once all the food had been taken I was left alone. Crawling back to my corner I lay down on what was left of my straw. Curling into a ball I tried to get some sleep.

After many restless hours the morning dawned bleak and drizzly. We were left with no information or instructions until mid-morning. At this point the servant girls from the night before came in with more bread, cheese and water. This time I shoved the food into my mouth, almost making myself retch in eagerness. Looking up I saw the man from last night watching me from beneath hooded eyes.

Again we were left.

Starting at midday, one by one our names were called. Once they left, none returned. Families, friends and loved ones were separated like cattle going for slaughter. I watched as a child clung to his mother, crying desperately not to be taken away. A marshal walked up to her, grabbed the child around the chest and dragged him away as his mother wept.

Half of the room had emptied when the girls were back with more bread, cheese and water.

More hours followed the same.

A low sun was casting long shadows as it streamed through the grimy windows when finally my name was called. The marshal from yesterday was back for me. His voice rang through the hall, "Clara Elizabeth Forge."

After a day of waiting my time had finally come. As I stood my muscles weakened, my heart pounding to the beat of an unheard drum. The holding room felt a mile long, my feet becoming heavier with every step I took as I walked towards the marshal.

"They're ready for you."

We walked back the way we had come yesterday. He led me up the side staircase and walked me deep into the building. The same oil lamps hung low along the corridor and it held the same varnished oak floor and doors. The last of the evening's rays filtered through the high windows, throwing my shadow long and ghostlike across the walls as I walked.

We eventually came to a large door with an ornate rose knocker. He knocked three times, opened the door and pushed me inside. I fell to my knees. Slowly my eyes worked their way over the roughly varnished floor, rising to the highly polished shoes of men among legs of mismatched chairs, finally coming to rest at a group of severe-looking men all dressed in what appeared to be their Sunday best.

The large man nearest me was holding a pocket watch in his hand, looking at it through a monocle. His booming voice filled the room, "You are late; you were supposed to be here yesterday at 12 o' clock sharp. Tell me, are you tardy, or have no perception of time?" His loud, harsh voice reverberated around the room as the other men glared at me accusingly.

Words failed me as I looked up at them. I could feel myself shrinking, retreating further into myself.

"Speak girl! Why are you here?" His brows furrowed in anger as he glowered down at me.

"I, my, its, my sister, she, she died, and, and, then. My mother, she was not well. She, uh, she died too. I have no one left. A family friend brought me here."

"A friend?" one of the men enquired with false intrigue.

"Yes, his name's Ned. He's…"

"And he couldn't care for you?" asked another.

"He tried, but he couldn't, I don't think he could afford it," I whispered. My eyes fell to the floor once more, to the scrapes in the varnish from the chairs being dragged and pulled across the floor during meeting just like this.

"So we must keep you? Let me ask you, do you think it fair that we take up the cost?"

"I, I don't know. I didn't want to come here. I was made to come here," I stammered.

"Are you saying this, free establishment, is not good enough for you?"

"No, no. I didn't mean that. I, I. I just…"

"I take it you want food and accommodation?" one of them interrupted again.

"Please, I have nowhere else to go; I have no one to go to," I begged.

"If you want such things you must work for such things!"

A man was sat at the back of the table; leaning back he folded his arms across his chest. "We could do with a new maid for the sewing room. The last one went to the infirmary last week; I had word this morning that she passed away during the night. She could take over her responsibilities?" he enquired. Picking up a glass of amber liquid, he rolled it thoughtfully as he inhaled.

The master of the workhouse looked to the back of the table. "Admit her, sort her and get her to work." He banged his meaty fist on the table, sealing my fate.

The men got up and shuffled out of the room, leaving the administrator to fill out the required paperwork. He asked my name, age, where I had lived and what I had done; he wanted the history of my life and did not seem content with the explanation I had given for my father's absence. He carefully detailed my belongings. Thankfully this did not take long as it consisted of a skirt, a shirt and the piece of rope I had used for many years as a belt. The questions continued for over an hour. Each reply I gave was judiciously noted down.

Once he was satisfied with the information I had given he went to the door and asked the marshal to escort me to the next area. The scribe left the room like the others had, as if I was no more than a smear of dirt on an otherwise sparkling floor.

"She is ready for processing," he confirmed to the marshal as he walked past.

The marshal pointed down a narrow corridor, "down there to the end, turn right, second door on the left. After you." He had an unsettling smile on his face.

When I reached the door in question I pushed it open. I was greeted by a barren room. It contained nothing more than a metal tub filled with water and a bar of soap on the floor. The only thing to break up the dirty brick walls were a few lonely shelves set high on the wall.

The marshal stood behind me, waiting expectantly. "Well hurry up, get rid of that stuff and get in before the doctor gets here."

"But you're still in here," I croaked, looking from him to the bath as I bit the inside of my mouth.

"Yes I am," he replied, "I'm here for your safety, gotta keep the girls safe," he added mockingly.

A dirty grin stretched across his face as he jangled the keys in his pocket. I was locked in. I had no choice but to do as he asked. He watched hungrily as I stripped naked, his gaze reminded me of Johns, hungry, predatory. I tried to cover myself as I stepped into the bitterly cold water. Sharp spasms of pain crawled under my skin and worked their way up my legs; the only thing worse than the aching pain was having him watch me. I dipped myself up to my chest and started scrubbing as fast as I could, wanting nothing more than my clothes back and my dignity restored.

The marshal sauntered over to the bath. I instinctively crouched over as his eyes swept the length of my body. He bent down, smiling at me with his sick smile, his fatty cheeks ruddy with sick excitement. He picked up my clothes and walked out, locking the door behind him. I sat in the bath, terrified, not knowing what to do.

He soon came back, looking quizzically at me. "You still not finished?" he raised his eyebrows and indicated with his chin, "out you get. The doctor's here."

I stepped out of the bath, completely humiliated.

"Stand," he ordered.

The marshal took a pair of scissors from the high shelves and started hacking at my hair. He clipped it close to my head, leaving no piece longer than an inch. It fell to the floor in dirty blonde waves, settling at my feet. I felt a few strands stick to my damp skin before they fell with the rest, each small tickle a reminder of what I was losing. I stood in the middle of the room, my body quacking with cold and humiliation. As I looked at the floor dry sobs were caught behind my clamorous teeth; I had no more tears left to cry. All of who I had once been had been ripped savagely away, I was just an object to these people.

There was a knock at the door; the marshal stepped away, admiring his work. He lazily walked over and unlocked the door, admitting who I hoped was the doctor.

"Right, let's have a look then," a well-bred man said as he stepped through the door. The doctor looked at my body appraisingly, lifting my arms and chin to check different areas. He was talking to himself, making notes on a board as he walked in a slow circle around me. "Skin damage to hands and knees, with scrapes to top left foot. Good weight, no sign of malnutrition. Slight abrasion to left forehead, wound appears relatively fresh," he noted as he gave it a hard prod for good measure. "Shows no outward signs of smallpox, typhoid nor any other common ailment or parasite. Recommendation: Start work, immediately." he looked at the marshal. "Get her dressed, get her to work."

Chapter 5

The marshal stepped up to me, dropping a grey dress at my feet as the doctor left the room. I picked it up and pulled it over my head, glad to be covered once more. With a tilt of his head he gestured for me to follow him. We walked out of the building, towards the segregation blocks. The labourers were split into four groups: The infirmary; the adult women, adult men and children between six and fourteen. Each block was exactly like the one before; ten windows wide, three stories high.

Finally we came to the children's quarter. He unlocked the door and ushered me inside. There were children everywhere, running, hiding, crying, the halls were in the constant grip of chaos and disruption. The rooms were full with urchins spilling from every crevice, the raucous screaming echoing through the corridors. We walked past room after room, all teeming with life. As we passed the children stopped, silence descending as the marshal walked. I saw the children's terrified glances when they saw him, barely daring to look. We stopped outside a nondescript cubby hole. It looked like it had once been a cupboard, turned into lodging due to a lack of space. Looking in I doubted I would be able to stand up straight whilst inside. I felt instantly dubious of many of us they would try to fit in.

"This is your room. You are in block 'a', level two and are in room 256b. Remember this, I will not tell you again."

I nodded my head, looking dispassionately at my new housing. Inside were two children. Both appeared to be around the same age as me. The girl was shy. I could see her making fretful glances at me whilst refusing to meet my eye; her brunette hair was just long enough to cover her bright green eyes. The boy was a lot bolder. He looked at me through a thick mop of jet black hair and gave me a blazing smile. He was the first child I had seen who did not wither at the marshals cutting glare. He took a swing at the boy, catching him across the ear with a snarl cracking through his lips.

"Follow me," he said, turning to glare at me. "I'll show you where you'll be working. You can clean? Can't you?"

I glared at him silently. He rubbed his chin thoughtfully, a sinister glint in his eye, before stepping back out of the small room and marching down the corridor. "Come," he called.

We walked to the end of the passage and down a flight of tightly winding stone steps. At the bottom we were faced with another identical hallway. He opened the first door we came to. There were rows upon rows of hard backed wooden chairs, each with a wicker basket on the floor in front of it, full of rags.

"You have been appointed to be the cleaning maid of this room. You are to clean it daily; it is your responsibility to ensure that I not find one piece of dirt. As long as you complete this task to my satisfaction you will be fed and watered sufficiently. Punishment for insubordination is restriction of food for a minimum of two days. The law states that any woman or child will not be beaten." He gave a sneering smirk as he checked his pocket watch. "It's time for supper. Go back the way we came and up three flights of stairs, the meeting hall is first on the right. You will then return to your room until day break where you will begin morning routine." He turned on his heel, leaving me stood in the middle of the empty room.

I slowly made my way back up the staircase, wondering how my life had changed so much and so fast. I may have been poor and my life had been hard, but my life had been my own. Now I was owned by the institution. A wave of resentment crashed over me. I wanted to rebel, in even the smallest of gestures. Looking superstitiously over my shoulder I decided to go to my new room.

As I approached the door I could hear the two children playing inside, I could not make out the game but the girl was giggling. As I reached the threshold the girl's laugh broke off abruptly. As I stepped through the door the boy jumped up and bounded over to me. His dark brown eyes sparkled as he wrung out my hand. I smiled back, trying to match his high-spirited welcome.

"Hi, I'm Will and this is Mary. So what's your name? You here with your family? What you in for? You been in before?"

He did not give me a chance to answer one of his questions, let alone all four, his strong northern accent causing the words to fall into one another.

"I'm Clara," I eventually managed. Before he jumped back in with more questions I leapt ahead of him, "I'm here because I had no other choice, my family are, they're gone, and no, I have not been in a workhouse before," I finished, managing to keep the turmoil rolling within me at bay. I was determined to keep everyone at arm's length; I could see nothing to be gained from getting close to anyone, especially not in here.

"So, same old same old," he replied with a casual shrug of his shoulders.

I looked at him quizzically.

"Same old story, every kid in here has lost someone, or everyone. All we got left is each other."

I freed my hand from his welcoming handshake and wrapped my arms around myself. I was huddled by the wall, my eyes sweeping the floor, trying to think of something to say, when a loud bell rang through the corridors.

"Come on, that means supper's ready." He turned to Mary who had not uttered a word since my arrival. "Gosh Mary, stop being so silly, she's gonna be living with us, you'll see, it'll be fine." He turned back to me. "Don't mind her, she'll come round. Just takes her a while to warm to people."

He walked over to Mary, took her by the hand and led her past me. As he got to the door he looked back. "You coming or what?"

I scooted forward and followed him up another flight of stairs to the dining hall. As we walked more and more children joined the throng moving to take their seats at the long benches. I sat down beside Will and hunched over the table, my arms folded across my chest, determined not to draw attention to myself. Mary quietly scurried to Will's other side. I kept my eyes on the table as the room filled around us.

There was a top table where four marshals stood, each in front of a different feeding station. The large man who had interviewed me earlier that day stepped into the hall. He was dressed immaculately, his grey three piece suit and matching hat preened to perfection. As he walked he pulled a gold watch from a pocket, flicking it open with the push of a concealed button. After a cursory glance he pushed the watch back into his pocket and sealed his hands behind his back, his large belly proudly pushed forwards as he stepped to the middle of the table. Everyone fell silent; you could hear a single toe scuff the floor, the bench creak under the children's weight. He did not utter a word but bowed his head and waited. In unison the children chanted:

"Be present at our table, Lord, Be here and everywhere adored. Thy creatures bless and grant that we May feast in paradise with Thee. Amen."

He gestured for us to stand. In neat rows the children lined up to collect their food. I kept behind Will the entire time, copying him so I would not stand out. As I reached the front of the queue the first marshal handed me a tray which held a plate, bowl, a cup full of water and a spoon. The second ladled broth into my bowl, the third gave me a hunk of bread and the forth a small block of cheese. I sat down in my allotted seat and ate my cold, bland food. Once everyone had finished we again sat in silence while some girls collected the plates. The master of the workhouse then bowed his head and the children chanted:

"Lord, behold our family here assembled. We thank you for this place in which we dwell, For the love that unites us, For the peace accorded to us this day, For the hope with which we expect the morrow; For the health, the work and the food; Amen."

The workhouse master stood and raised his hands, "Dismissed!"

When we got back to our room Will and Mary walked in and sat down in areas that had obviously been allocated a long time ago. I stayed on the threshold, leaning on the door frame, picking at my nail beds and dry skin. Eventually Will looked up. "What you doing out there?" he asked with a crooked smile. "Come on, in you get."

I looked to the small space beside him and he shifted over to give me more room, patting the area with his hand.

Folding myself onto the patch a straw Will watched Mary dig deep into the straw next to where she was sitting. I looked from her to Will, hoping one of them was going to offer an explanation. Will smiled at me but said nothing while his excitement grew like that of a small child at Christmas.

Eventually Mary picked something out of the dirt and held it in her hand. She smiled shyly up at Will who was now twitching with anticipation. "Good job Mary, let's see them!"

She handed over the mystery objects and Will held them up so they were caught in the light from the lantern burning low in the hall.

"Are they marbles!?" I asked, not believing what I was seeing.

"Yeah, found them the other day. Have no idea where they came from, just found them in the corridor last week. You wanna play?"

"I've never played with real marbles before. Only some old clay ones my mother…" I stopped, unable to finish the sentence.

Will gazed at me, his eyes wide with pained understanding. He recovered himself before I had a chance to reassemble my thoughts. "Here, have a look, look at the colors."

He handed me the cool rocks and I held them to the light, examining them closely. They were a reddish-brown with black flakes that sparkled as they the light hit them. "Look at that," I said turning them to and fro.

"Alright, enough with the pretty patterns!" he laughed.

I giggled as I handed over the stones and we began to play.

That night I lay on my bed of straw, running through everything that had happened to me and my family. My father missing, my deceased sister and my mother lost to the shadow lands. Ned had now abandoned me. I was alone. Here, I was just a number. As Will put it, 'same old, same old.' As discontent itched its way over my body I rolled over and prayed for sleep to take me, to escape this place for just a few precious hours.

The next morning dawned bright and early. I had overslept. Will was dragging me to my feet while I was still half asleep. "Come on, we'll be late for Morning Prayer!"

It went very similarly to the night before. We chanted the Lord's Prayer, had a breakfast of bread and gruel, followed by a prayer of thanks. I was about to get up to leave when Will stopped me. Placing his hand on top of mine he ushered me to sit.

Unbeknown to me morning routine consisted of three hours of teaching. A somber woman entered the hall; she was to be our teacher for the day. She was small and mouse-like, almost wilting in the way she stood, with fast, shaky movements. Looking at her I seriously doubted her merits as a tutor. The first hour was learning new prayers for the week and reciting the Lord's Prayer word for word perfectly. Her muted voice echoed through the silent hall, making it sound indistinct and ghostlike. The second hour was numeracy. She taught us one to ten and then started on ten to twenty. When she was not looking our way I leaned over and whispered to Will, "Do these lessons get any harder? I could count to ten by the age of nine!"

"I would love to make you feel better and say yes, but I can't. They won't teach us no more coz the teachers don't know no more," he whispered back.

Once we had completed the task of counting to twenty the last hour was given to literacy. This was of far more use to me. I had been taught to count through the necessity of handling money but I had never been taught to read or write. All I had ever learnt was what I had taught myself. The lesson today was letters. We went through the alphabet and by the end of the hour I could recite it with only a few mistakes.

We finished our lessons and peeled off in different directions to our respective trades. I entered the sewing room to find some children already hard at work. Looking down I could see a faint layer of dust covering the floor. As the light shone in from the large windows I could see where the children walked in and out, always following the same path; a slight indent in the floor from years of children's tired, heavy feet treading the same boards day in, day out. I found my cleaning supplies in the storeroom and started scrubbing the floor. I repeated it again and again up and down until I heard the lunch bell chiming.

I got to my feet and started packing away my supplies. By the time I was organized I was the last one to leave. I started walking towards the door when the marshal came in.

"No, no, no," he said snaking his head from side to side in malicious humor. "I don't think this is clean enough at all," he continued in mock sadness, his slack jowls that hung from the sides of his face trembling as he spoke. Slowly he paced into the room. I watched, my jaw quivering as he licked a dro p of spit from his lower lip, his tongue following of the dry, cracked line. I dropped his gaze and stared at the floor. I saw his boots; they were coated in wet dirt. Each step he took left a muddy print and small pieces of muck were falling between footfalls, marking his tail like blackened breadcrumbs.

He stopped before me. Slowly he rubbed his boots on my clean floor, a snarling laugh escaping his lips. He raised his hand and slapped me.

Chapter 6

Ever since my run-in with the marshal on my second day I made sure I always had company. I remember crying myself to sleep that night. I had been left with a bloodied lip and swollen cheek. Will showed me great kindness; finding a clean rag he dabbed gently at my lip, wiping the blood from my face before dipping the blood stained rag into a dish of cool water and holding it to my eye. That was the night I began to trust again. He had spent the night trying to ease my pain, telling me the sorry story of his life.

He was lying on his side, looking at me through the darkness, my eyes now used to the muted light. "Me Ma' and Pa' couldn't find no work, that's how we came to being in here. We started as miners," he explained. "I was one of fourteen." Will rolled onto his back and, gazing into the darkness, began recalling what happened to his family. "Seven of them died down the mines, one blast took four at one time, the whole tunnel caved in, you see. Another brother and my sister, they drowned. She fell in the lake, she shouldn't have been anywhere near the water," he spat bitterly. "Rob went in after her and neither of them came out. The other four, well, none of them lived past the age of two." He rolled back so he was looking at me once more. "When I was the only one left me Ma' and Pa' thought we could do with a change, something a bit safer; only problem was they couldn't find no work. No work, no money. No money, no food. Didn't take long after getting in here before Ma' died of something, they never told me what, just told me she was dead. And Pa' got in a fight that went bad for him. And now… now it's just me."

"I'm sorry," I whispered.

"Nothing to be done by it now." He paused, just looking at me, before a small, regretful smile lifted his cheeks. "So, what's your story then?" Will asked gruffly. "You don't have to tell me if you don't want to," Will muttered as he watched my face change.

"No, it's okay. It's just." I looked back at him, trying to clear the moisture from my eyes. "My dad disappeared a while ago now. Left to find work and never came back." Breaking his eye contact I picked up a piece of straw and started picking it apart with cold fingers. "Then my sister got sick. She died. After that, my mum just faded away. She's dead too."

Will said nothing. After an age he nodded.

"What about her?" I asked, pointing with my chin to Mary, Will's silent, ever-present shadow.

"Dunno. She never told me." He shrugged and looked at her, his face crumpled in confused concern. "Takes a while to come round to stuff, but she's alright."

Over the weeks that followed Mary came to trust me. She had started uttering the odd word in my direction and after a few months all of our barriers had disintegrated. We were a family, they were my family. Will and I had quickly become close; he was the light that diminished my shadow. His quick wit reminded me of my sister and his zeal for life kept both mine and Mary's spirits high, especially during the darker times.

The death and departure of children turned the workhouse into a factory of souls rather than commodities. Outside of our trio it was almost impossible to make friends. The children got sick, had accidents, aged out or were removed by their parents.

One thing that had not changed however was my place in the workhouse. To keep myself safe I would begin clearing away my supplies shortly before the bell tolled. Leaving with the other girls I would be easily lost in the crowd. This had worked for a while; until today. The marshal was waiting for me.

I looked up to see him leaning on the door frame, watching me, a sadistic smile playing across his thin lips. I knew I was not supposed to pack my things away before the bell rang but if I waited he would have me alone. I spent the rest of the morning trying to think of a way to avoid our encounter but I was quickly running out of time. Every time I looked up dread would wash over me once more, his cold, calculating eyes never moving from me.

The bell tolled and with it my heart sank. As all the children dropped their sewing and started to leave I tried to catch someone's eye. Thankfully a girl locked eyes with me.

"Excuse me? Could you help me put my things away please?" I asked, imploring the girl with my eyes.

She glanced at the marshal before giving me a remorseful look, dropping her eyes she walked on in silence. She had seen this before, they all had, they knew what was going to happen.

I worked as fast as I could to pack away the supplies. Snatching my bucket and cloth I ran to the cupboard, slamming the door shut in my urgency. I stilled, absorbing the silence I turned to face him.

He stalked me, calculating his every step. I stood paralyzed in my fear, knowing there was no one to come to my aid. No family, no friend or tainted knight to save me.

He stood before me, waiting. When I did not move he extended a thin finger, curling it slowly, beckoning me forwards. Knowing what was about to happen I stepped towards him, dropping my eyes to the floor. Again he curled his finger, this time leaning forward like he was encouraging a dog that had been beaten once too often.

I walked forwards until I was directly in front of him. Then he hit me. I stood, frozen, as he hit me again and again, the painful slap ringing through my face causing my skin to blaze. Finally I fell, unable to take it.

"Up!" he barked, "I said UP!" he roared as he took my hair in his fist and dragged me to my feet.

Once more the blows began to fall.

Again I fell.

"Did I say I was finished?" he hissed in my ear. I felt his spit hit my cheek, the tiny drops landing on my bloodied lips.

"No," I whimpered.

"Then why are you on the floor?" he sneered.

"Please, no more, please," I cried.

My pleading went unheard as the beating continued.

By the time he was finished I was covered in a patchwork of bruises ranging from slightly reddened skin to hard, purple-black fist imprints. He had laughed, telling me he had to make up for lost time. I missed lunch; he only stopped when the children returned. Despite my aching ribs and battered body I took out my cleaning supplies and continued with my afternoon's work. I would not go to the infirmary. Many went in, but few ever came out.

As the girls began trickling back into the room I looked into the eyes of the one who had refused to come to my aid. I saw the sorrow in her eyes as she walked past. I kept my eyes to the floor for the rest of the day, wiping away my tears as they fell to the floor.

Thankfully the marshal did not return that evening, leaving me free to go to supper. As I walked into the dining hall Will clocked my face. His expression became rigid, his eyes wide, as he stared at me. He got off the bench and ran to me. We stood as long as we dared, his shirt becoming wet with the tears I shed against his chest. He led me to our bench, watching every step I took.

"What happened to you?" He was distraught as he looked over me, surveying the damage.

"It's nothing," I dismissed

He glared at me.

"It's the marshal. You know what he's like. He managed to get me on my own again." I looked down at my knees, feeling the disgrace wash over me.

"It's gonna be okay. Just stay with me 'til I come up with something," he said as he looked around, scouting the area for any sign of the marshal in question.

Mary reached over and took my hand, rubbing it with her thumb. We sat holding hands as we recited our prayers. Will ushered me to the front table with him to collect our food. When we sat down he passed me his bread, giving me an encouraging, sad smile. We ate in silence, not bothering to whisper behind our hands as we normally did. I could feel Will's temper rising the longer we sat and by the end of the meal his anger was palpable.

When we got back to our room he detonated. "Who does he think he is? Someone should do something about him. Just look at you! They all know he does it, but none of them even try to stop him!"

"Will, there is nothing anyone can do. They run this place, he runs this place. They have control over everyone and everything. I'm fine; honestly, it looks a lot worse than it is. Please calm down," I tried to placate.

He was sat cross legged on the floor, pummeling the dirt with his fist. "No! You are not alright. It looks like he's kicked you from one end of the room to the next. What you gonna do tomorrow?" he looked up at me, glaring defiantly.

I folded my arms defensively across my bruised chest. "I'll think of something," I finally replied lamely, refusing to meet his eye.

After a minute of awkward silence I saw a spark of hope dance across Will's face. "You don't have to; I've already got an idea. I'll skip out of stone breaking early and meet you before lunch. I'll be waiting at the door for you. I'll stand right next to the marshal if I have to."

"As much of an amazing idea that it is, I don't think it's going to work."

"Why not?"

"Well, first of all you have to get past the marshals in control of your area."

"Easy, I'll tell them I've hit me leg with the hammer and need to go to the infirmary. I'll just limp really badly, they won't question it," he said, shrugging my concerns aside.

"That is one of the worst excuses I've ever heard. And yes, they will question it!" I interjected.

"Fine, I will hit myself in the leg with the hammer!" he said, now laughing at my obvious irritation.

"That is not the only flaw in your master plan," I said rolling my eyes at his mocking, dismissive attitude. "How are you going to get past all the other marshals?"

"I'll tell them I have a message that I can only deliver to the marshal at your end. I'll tell them I'm sworn to secrecy," he replied with a nonchalant wave of his hand.

"I don't even know where to start with the holes in that part of your plan!" I groaned, throwing my hands in the air and looking to Mary for help.

"Don't bother." Will held up his hand to silence Mary as she opened her mouth. "It'll work. I'll be there before lunch tomorrow," Will finished, his hand still raised to stop Mary from interjecting.

"Look, there is no point! He may not even be there tomorrow and you would have risked two days of food for nothing. Please let's just forget the whole thing."

He dropped it for the evening but I knew him well enough to know I would not have discouraged him from his insane plot. That night when we lay on the straw Mary and Will were asleep in minutes. I was not so lucky. The marshals beating had taken its toll on my body and I could find no comfort in the straw. I was resigned to a long and painful night.

The workhouse was quiet, not even a cry to be heard rolling through the cold night, when out of the darkness I heard Will's quiet sigh.

"Still not comfy?" he grumbled softly.

"You are supposed to be asleep," I whispered back.

"I would be if someone stopped fidgeting for more than three minutes," he retorted.

"I have been still for more than three minutes thank you!" I whispered in mock aggravation.

"No you haven't, I've been counting. Your longest has been two minutes and fifty three seconds, if my counting's accurate."

"Well it's your counting, so probably not," I sniggered.

I heard him laugh in response. "Come here," he said as he shuffled closer to me.

He lifted his arm and I snuggled up to him, my head resting on his chest. I may have been aching all over but I felt better for being close to him. Finally I fell into a restful sleep.

The next day went just as Will said it would. Before the lunch bell rang he was stood inside the door, waiting for me. I smiled when I noticed him there, looking cocky at his obvious triumph. Suddenly the shadowy figure of the marshal loomed behind him. My smile fell as my eyes came to rest upon him. He started talking to Will. I could see Will shaking his head, his feet planted firmly on the floor. Before the marshal could take further action the bell tolled the repeated ring echoing through the silent room. Will turned away from the marshal and bounded over to me, an ecstatic expression on his face. As he bent down to help me with my supplies he whispered in my ear, "told you it would work!"

I did not dare look up, sensing the marshal was still there. We busied ourselves with tidying the area and only when the room was completely clear did I look to see the doorway standing open and empty. Will was giddy with delight; we had beaten the marshal at his sick game. We walked up the stairs in high spirits. When we met Mary at the lunch table Will told her the story in great detail. Mary initially looked impressed with Will, but when his attention was drawn elsewhere she leaned forward and gave me a worried look. She was thinking along the same lines as me. This would not work for long; the marshal would not stand for being beaten.

The next day went the same as the last. Just before lunch Will appeared at the door, standing proudly on the threshold; the marshal did not. As the bell rang Will sauntered over to me, his hands deep in his pockets. "See, that's all it needed. Bet he'll never bother you again."

"I don't know," I replied, still concerned. "Doesn't it seem just a little too easy?"

"Na, he's a coward. Trust me he won't come near you anymore."

We made our way into the lunch hall and scanned for Mary. She was nowhere to be seen.

"Where could she have gone? She's never late," Will muttered, checking and rechecking the hall to see if we had somehow missed her.

We ate our meal in silence, privately contemplating where our friend could be. After lunch we returned to our work. I tried to reassure Will that she would be fine but I could see the worry etched into his furrowed brow as we parted for the afternoon.

I worked through the evening until supper. As the bell chimed I looked up to see Will waiting for me by the door. As I walked towards him I could see his concern for Mary had deepened. He was transferring his weight from foot to foot. As soon as I came level with him he turned and we made our way to the hall, shouldering our way through the growing crowd in our haste.

As we rushed into the hall it did not take Will long to spot Mary over the other children's heads, anxiously pointing her out at the far end. She was sat alone, far removed from the other children. Will and I ran to her side. She brushed us away, shaking her head as a single tear ran down her bruised cheek. We sat protectively on either side of her.

"What happened?" I asked.

Mary's bottom lip quivered, causing a wound she had sustained to ooze. A single drop of blood clung to the delicate skin of her lip as she stuttered uncontrollably. She took a deep, steadying breath to compose herself. Finally she turned to Will. "He said to tell you that you can't protect us both." Her voice was loud but shaky, exposing her hurt and humiliation.

Will sat in shock; words abandoning him as the gravity of her statement settled and took root in his mind. We sat in silence, starring numbly at our forgotten food, before walking back to our room.

"What are we going to do?" Will asked, finally breaking the silence that had consumed our pitiful sleeping quarters.

Neither of us answered. We were stuck in this world for at least three years. We all knew how it worked, once orphaned you could not discharge yourself until you were sixteen. Will was nearly fourteen, I had only just turned thirteen and Mary was eleven.

"We have to get out of this place!" Will shouted into the silence.

"How?" I asked, the word resonating in the small space sounded harsher than intended.

"I don't know," he replied, throwing the clump of dirt he had been toying with against the wall.

Despite Will's best efforts the cruelty continued. Mary and I took it in turns to be the focus of the marshal's mad vendetta. I knew if Mary had been beaten one day, I would be next. Waiting anxiously as the clock ticked towards 12 o' clock, I would stare at the door, waiting for the knob to turn, waiting for him to walk in. As the months passed the torture continued, an escape plan never coming to light.

I was working one afternoon when I heard the marshal shouting for everyone on our floor to line up. As usual I was the last one in the procession, clearing away my supplies before I left. I poked my head around the door to see everyone lining up along the corridor. I could see a lot of fearful glances being thrown to one another.

I followed suit, lining up with my back pressed against the wall. We took our customary stance, head down, eyes to the floor. The marshal walked down the line, thrashing his cane through the air. The hum and thwack as it hit the floor just missing our bare toes made us all wince. We dared not move. He turned and marched back up the line, bellowing in our faces, daring us to flinch. All too soon it became clear what had happened.

We had received a new high table since the old one was beyond repair. Upon inspection this morning he had noticed a mark in the varnish. He was determined to find the guilty party.

"Whoever committed this crime step forward. NOW!" the marshal bellowed.

No one moved.

"I will beat every single child here until I find you. Announce yourself and spare your friends the indignity of what will befall them at your cowardice," he thundered, his face a mere inch from the child he was harrying.

Still no one moved. The marshal marched to the end of the line.

"I will start with you," he growled, shoving the tip of his cane into a boy's chest. "Turn and bare your back."

One after another the children were beaten. Some stood still as they cried out in pain; others flinched away, trying to protect themselves. I glanced down the aisle and saw Will was next. As the marshal came level with him he gave the order. "Turn and bare your back."

Will squared his shoulders, looked him straight in the eye and declared loud enough for everyone to hear, "I know nothing of this, Sir. I did not do it!"

The marshal glared at him, the evil glint in his eye magnified by his thick glasses. "Enough of this! Down with your clothes!"

"No! I won't let you, not again!"

The words had scarcely passed his lips. The marshal took him by the collar and thrust him against the wall, kicking him until he slid to the floor. Rolling onto his back Will gasped for air. Reaching down the marshal dragged him up by the back of his neck and threw him to the floor once more.

Will reached out his hands and started crawling away from the marshal; blood dripping from his mouth as he heaved the air into his lungs. The marshal stalked him down the hallway like a predator. He stood above him, his cruel laughter reverberating off the walls of the silent corridor. Will rolled onto his back; an enraged cry escaping his lips.

As the marshal bent down to strike him Will brought up the heel of his foot and smashed it into the marshal's face. He reeled backwards, screaming in agony. The marshal's glasses had been shattered, the glass splinters blinding him. Will clambered to his feet, took the cane and started beating the marshal; beating every part of his body he could reach as hard as he could. His hand holding the cane rose high in the air and stilled, holding for two harrowing breaths, before falling upon the marshal's body once more. He screamed and roared as he attacked; like a dam, finally able to burst its banks, he let go of the anger, the sadness and the frustration he had been forced to hold on to for so long.

When his strength finally left him he looked up, His breathing heavy, labored. I could see small flecks of blood covering his face and body. With a clatter that echoed through the silent corridor the cane fell to the floor. Everyone stood in stunned silence. The marshal lay unmoving, his lips no longer drawing breath, his eyes no longer searching out there next victim. His arms were spread wide as his bleeding, half-closed eyes stared blankly towards the wall. Will just stood over him, looking dazed.

Unsteady, I stepped out of the line. "This is bad. This is very bad. We've got to get out of here. Will. COME ON! RUN!"

I grabbed Will by the arm and took Mary by the hand. Together we ran down the corridor, ran away from the body. We had to escape before another marshal found it.

* * *

I stop and drop my pen as my heart pounds to the beat of the drums. I can feel the fear of that moment. The memory is still crystal clear in my mind. I can still see the way Will stood as he looked down upon the marshal. I can still see the tiny flakes of blood that smattered his body, the bright crimson drops like ink staining his skin.

I am pulled from my book as someone walks in, his face lost in the shadows.

"How are we looking?"

"I don't know how much longer it's going to take," I answer.

"They're only now loading up the boat, you still have time."

He turns to leave, stopping in the threshold, his head bowed, not looking at me. "Write from your heart Clara."

I refill my dip pen and press the tip to the parchment once more. The words, once more, begin their scrawling journey across the page as I unburden my heart.

Chapter 7

We tore down the corridor. As we reached the end I heard shouting coming from behind us. They had found him. Before I ran through the door I looked back to see the children pointing in our direction. Men were already running after us. We ran down the stairs, along another corridor and burst through the front doors. The bright summer sun blinded me, my hands rising to block out the painful glare. Running out of time we sprinted into the light. Marshals poured from every door. They were shouting to one another, joining into ever increasing groups, forming a line, a human barricade. They were quickly surrounding us, cutting off all possible exits.

There were only a few gaps left. We ran for an opening. As I darted past a marshal's fingers skimmed my arm. We may have got past the guards but the complex was surrounded by an impenetrable brick wall. I looked for a climbable area as I ran but it was sheer red brick, not a foot hold in sight. I spun around to see men closing in on us from all sides; they knew we could not escape. When they caught us we would pay for what we had done.

Will took my arm and dragged me sideways, Mary already ahead of us. We ran around the back of the buildings, the air becoming cooler as we found our way into the shadows. The marshals had lost sight of us. I could hear them shouting to one another, they were hunting us like a pack of dogs, the smell of blood thick in their nose. We darted behind some discarded barrels as a marshal ran past. As the air stilled we crept out before running on again. As we rounded the corner Will picked up the pace.

"This way," Will called.

Looking up I could see where he was taking us. At the far end there was a wrought iron gate. We ran to the gateway, crashing into it in our haste to get to the other side.

"What is this?" I asked as I dragged the air into my lungs.

"Dunno. I've only seen it from the windows, figured it's got to be the back door."

"Let's hope so," I said as we struggled with the chain that fastened it to the wall.

Mary rocked from foot to foot as the sound of the marshals hunt reached our ears once more. I gripped the bars and pulled the gate towards us as Will tried to free it from the chain.

"Quick, they're coming," Mary cried, pushing herself i nto the wall as she pointed to the far end of the compound. "They're coming!"

Suddenly the chain slackened a fraction and I pushed the gate back. The gap was tiny.

"Mary, you first," Will said, putting his weight against the gate.

Mary ducked and slipped through the narrow gap, her small frame fitting through it with ease.

"Clara, you next."

I looked behind, the marshals had slowed their pace, they knew we were trapped. "Go go go," Will hissed.

"But Will," I tried to turn to him.

"Go!" he shouted, pushing at the door, the hinges protesting with whining groans. He looked back at the marshals. "Now, quick."

Mary was on the other side, pulling at the solid bars. I knelt down and pushed myself through the narrow gap, feeling the metal pressing against my front and the rough stone grating against my back. Scrambling to my knees I joined Mary, pulling on the gate as Will tried to get to us.

He turned his head and slid through the gap to his shoulders. With Mary and me dragging on the rusted iron structure he reached his arms through and using them to push back on the bars, dragged his body the rest of the way. His feet caught on the rungs in his haste and were barely past when Mary and I rammed the gate closed. Will dragged himself to his feet and started twisting the chain, retightening it as the marshals surrounded us.

We stepped back from the gate as their arms reached through, desperately trying to ensnare us in their brutal grasps. We were out of reach but when I looked up and saw where we were I almost collapsed, the air leaving my body as dread crept over me. We were surrounded by the high walls of the outer perimeter, in a ten foot square outhouse with nothing but old planks of haphazardly laid wood used to make a roof. I stumbled back, trying to find the wall with my hands, when I tripped over a grate. Looking down I saw we were above the sewage pit. All the waste from the workhouse was poured into it where it flowed into the Thames. I took a deep breath as a ridiculous idea flourished in my mind. I nudged Will with my elbow and pointed down, giving him a meaningful look.

"You have got to be kidding me!" he choked.

"Would you rather be hung?" I hissed. "Help me get this grate off!"

Mary quickly deduced what we were planning. Together we dragged the grate away from the opening. The marshals had got a key, they were unlocking the gate. The chain clanged as it was dragged through the iron bars. We had no time to consider our decision. Jumping as the marshals made their final advance, we landed in the stinking muck. It was thick with filth and the smell coating my mouth caused me to retch. Looking up I saw the marshals peering in at us. I looked ahead, into the all-encompassing darkness.

"Come on, it goes down that way," Will pointed, his voice distorting strangely in the echoing catacomb.

I started down the dark tunnel, Will and Mary following in my wake. The voices of the marshals were soon lost to the deep impenetrable darkness that engulfed us. I could see nothing. Eventually coming to the side of the tunnel I used it as a guide, always keeping one hand on the slimy rock, the other out behind me, holding on to Mary. Will stayed at the back, making sure we were not followed.

We waded further into the gloom; our heightened senses our only guide. The tunnel felt infinite, with no end to the labyrinthine sewers. The ducts we were wading through were constantly twisting, making violent turns as they joined another tunnel, the channels becoming larger the farther we travelled through the endless darkness.

In time the muck started to thin, it was mixing with fresh water. We continued on as the air became less stagnant. I could hear water from tiny tributaries joining our progress. A current began to ebb around us, pushing us further down the tunnel. With the push and pull of the water walking became more difficult. I started to lose my footing on the slippery bottom.

As we staggered on I saw light from an unknown source reflecting off the water. It was weak, flickering over the surface. Finally we rounded a corner and I could see a spot of light in the distance. The current carried us towards the glow, the small spot slowly growing bigger. The water was getting deeper, it was now up to my shoulders and there were moments when I would lose the floor completely.

I felt Mary pull urgently on my arm. Looking behind I saw her struggling, the dirty water lapping at her chin. I tried to get a firmer grip of her hand but the filth caused her desperately reaching fingers to slip through my numbed grasp. Will swam up to her just as her head sank below the dirty water, grabbing her under the arms he pulled her onto his chest. I gripped his arm and tried to guide him through the current.

We were now being pulled along, unable to control our speed or direction. The light was getting closer, the small spot now a great white expanse before us. I tried to swim against the current, tried to slow us down; we were going too fast. All of a sudden we were bathed in warm summer light.

I was blinded by the glare as we were swept out of the tunnel. As my eyes adjusted shadowy shapes loomed above me. My vision was dominated by huge boats that surrounded us. The current was dragging us towards a ship, its hard iron side looming above us. We were coming level; I could not fight the current carrying us to our death. I closed my eyes and waited for the impact.

I opened my eyes to see the ship drifting past. We had missed it by inches, its wake now pushing us further into the shipping lanes.

We may have forestalled the first blow but another was on the horizon. A large ship was fast approaching. We screamed for help. I saw people lean over the edge; pointing to us they hailed to others for help. Ropes appeared, dangling from the edge; they were lowering them into the water, making dummy throws to judge the distance. The vessel was slowing, trying to come close enough for us to catch the ropes whilst not drowning us in the undertow. As the ship drifted past we made frantic grabs at the ropes. Finally my hand made contact with one as it slapped the surface of the water.

As I gripped the rope with all my strength the men on board took in the slack. My body was jarred suddenly forwards before the rope abruptly slackened. Before I could take a breath my head was pulled under, the water engulfing my senses. In my panic I lost my grip on the rope, abandoned to the turbulent undercurrents.

I felt myself tumbling; saw flashes of light followed by darkness. My head collided with something hard as precious bubbles of air fell from my mouth. I swam for what I thought was the surface only to find my world becoming darker. My mind and ribs began a desperate battle. As my vision began to fade I felt myself take in mouthfuls of the invading water. My lungs screamed for air. Images faded in and out of focus. My mother's face, healthy and smiling, holding out her hand floated towards me. As she drifted away in the murky water I reached out my hand, trying desperately to reach her. Then it was my sister. Grace was not happy. She was shouting, trying to push me away. I tried to shout out to her but more water filled my mouth. I was deep under the water, being dragged further away by the deadly current. My sister was fading, I was losing her again. My world misted into darkness as the last bubbles of air left my lungs. The last image burning in my mind was that out my sister's furious face as I floated into oblivion.

Someone was slapping me on the back. I started coughing, my lungs burning in their need for air. Hacking up mouthfuls of dirty water I struggled onto my hands and knees before rolling onto my side as spasms hauled through my body. With my throat on fire and my chest heaving I looked upon my rescuers. I was surrounded by sailors. Casting my eyes further afield I could see a sopping wet Will with Mary clinging to his elbow. Both looked pale and shocked. A dozen hands reached out to me as I tried to get to my feet.

"Thanks," I coughed, my voice painful and husky.

The men nodded in reply, offering the odd word of sympathy.

"We're about to dock, you kids alright to get off here?" a man called from the front of the boat.

"That'll be fine thank you," Will said formally before turning to me. "Are you alright? When you didn't come up with us, I, I thought you were gone." He closed his eyes as pain washed over him. I had never seen him look so pained, so lost before.

"So did I for a moment." I tried to brush his concern aside, hiding my feelings behind a false smile. He did not need to be laboured with my fear. "Let's just get off this ship and work out what we're going to do next." I looked to the shore, pretending to admire a scenery I was blind to in my broken-down state.

As the boat started heading for the docks we stood awkwardly on the side of the boat. I could see the sailors looking at us, muttering to one another. Looking down I realised why. We were still in our workhouse uniforms and it was obvious we did not get into our current situation by any legal means. I tried to look inconspicuous, refusing to make eye contact. I prayed they did not ask us for payment, we had nothing to give.

Thankfully nothing came of my concern. No one spoke to us, offered us anything or asked anything of us. They lowered the gang plank and offered their hands to help us down. As Will hopped off the edge of the boat he turned to thank our rescuers.

The Captain lifted his hand to silence him. "We didn't see you and you didn't see us," he simply offered.

Maybe we were not the only ones trying to survive in the shadows.

Once off the boat we sat on the embankment, acclimatizing ourselves to our new surroundings. As the shock of what happened wore off I began to feel a chill creep over my body. I got to my feet, rubbing my arms to try and bring some warmth back into them. I surveyed our surroundings. I did not recognise a single structure around us. On the edge of the river banks were boats chained to moorings set further up the bank. I could see wading birds picking their way through the muck, looking for any morsels of food buried like treasure in the mud. Children were digging in the shallows, some up to their knees and elbows in the deep mud.

Leaving Will and Mary at the river bank I wandered up the bank to take a closer look at the buildings. I stumbled through the mud, using my hands as I slipped, losing my footing every other step. I struggled on until I came to the cobbled path that separated the buildings from the edge of the river bank. This part of London was made up of tall imposing structures with square brick walls and small windows. The one in front had a sign painted in red and blue. I used my new literacy skills to sound the words out loud.

"Dob…son's dis…till…ery? Dobson's Distillery!" I proudly announced to no one in particular.

"What's that?" Will asked, making me jump.

"It's where they make the alcohol."

Looking further afield I saw we were completely surrounded by industrial buildings. I could make out a furniture factory and a dye factory but the others were a mystery to me. Directly on my right was one of the largest structures I had ever seen. It had an open front with large planks of wood mounted on iron frames which ran from the structure down to the base of the river, eventually disappearing under the dark water. I looked at Will and saw an inquisitive gleam in his eye. Checking no one was watching we walked over, Mary creeping behind us. The closer we got the larger the structure became.

When we reached the slip-way I saw that the rivets holding the wood and metal structure together came up to my nose. I had never seen anything of this scale in my life. Looking inside I saw an incomplete ship. It was a patchwork of metal sheets, wooden frames, ropes and pulleys. The men working looked like ants scurrying about its broad surface. I could hear the men hollering to one another, calling for help and supplies. This was accompanied by a constant pounding as pieces of a giant jigsaw were forced into place.

Curiosity getting the better of us, we clambered onto the trail of wood and iron. I was immediately enthralled by what I could see. The sheer scale of the undertaking was breath-taking. I became lost in the intricate working of the men, all of what had just transpired being pushed to the back of my mind as I watched them work. As I looked on I became oblivious to my surroundings, eagerly edging closer to the building. I could feel the tension rolling off of Will as he stood behind me, obviously wanting to concentrate on more pressing matters.

"OI!"

I stopped in my tracks. A burly man was striding towards us from the top end of the ship yard.

"What do you mudlarks think you're doing?" the man hollered.

He was advancing on us, anger evident on his hardened face. We leapt down from the huge runners and ran away. Rounding a corner we found ourselves in a dark alleyway; the factories on either side obscuring the sun. The further we walked the lower the temperature dropped, the cold dark street quickly suppressing my thrilled heart. Slowly I began to take stock of what had happened and the situation we now found ourselves in. I looked to Will. "What are we going to do?"

"I think we need a change of clothes. I don't know about you but I'm freezing and if anyone sees us in these they'll know we came from a workhouse. When you leave by right you get given the clothes you arrived in. We can't be recognised as the kids who escaped from that place. I now have a price on my head. Come on."

Chapter 8

We followed Will as he jogged to the end of the alley, ran down a small street and took a series of random turns. He came to a sudden halt when we came around the last corner. There were people everywhere, the likes of which I had never seen before. I gaped as a woman walked towards me, her skin a slightly different colour to mine. It was nothing like the warm browns and sooty blacks of some of the people I had seen living in the murkier parts of Devils Acre, not at all, but it still seemed different. Her face heralded to a different world, her almond-shaped eyes perfectly framing her dark irises, her black hair in a high bun atop her head.

As I stepped back for her to pass I could not help myself. My hand rose and I ran the very tips of my fingers across the soft fabric of her dress, it was of brightest blue covered in hand woven trees and flowers. It wrapped around her body and was held in place with a thick, beautifully tied piece of black ribbon secured around her small waist. She stopped mid pace and turned to me. With a knowing look in her eye she smiled softly before bowing to us, her hands clasped in front of her, her head dipping slightly. I took a step back, my hand falling to my side as she walked on. Stumbling back further, craning my neck as she walked into the meandering crowd, my legs collided with a stall. I felt it rock precariously against my weight. I span around and clutched the side, terrified of incurring the wrath of an angry tradesman, only to see another strange person looking quizzically at me.

He was small, with white hair tied back in a ponytail. As I took a steadying breath the smell hit me. I looked down at the array of produce in front of me. There were small, light brown, rolled sticks all chopped to one uniform size, star shaped pods looking like Earths versions of stars, and seeds and blackish pods. The collection of spices filled the table, each in their own earthen bowl. I was tempted to pick some up, but past experience told me this would not be a good idea.

As I looked back to the man he smiled and gave me a small bow. Picking up a handful of seeds he pulled back the sleeves of his black smock and rubbed them in his hands before offering them to me. I looked at his small, wiry hands blankly. Smiling again he brought his hands to his face and inhaled before offering them to me. As I bent my head forward Will caught my elbow, urgently pulling me back. Looking up I pushed his hand away with a self-conscious smile.

I turned to follow Will but stopped once more when I saw Mary. She was standing stock still and staring ahead. I followed her gaze. People were dancing down the street. They were holding great paper structures of colourful monsters, raising them high above their heads before dipping them low. Instantly distracted I threw a cursory eye to Will.

I looked back towards the new manifestation dancing down the street. As it whirled closer towards us I began to hear the music. Some kind of flute was being played, soon to be joined by another and another and then another instrument merged in, picking out the accompanying notes like drops of crisp water from a free falling rain. I could see people stood below an enormous handmade monster, the bright, painted paper flashing vibrantly in the bright sun. It was held on sticks, each part of the body controlled by a different man. I felt my lips lift and a laugh spill from my lips as it danced in time to the music. They soared past us, swaying and swirling down the street, long ribbons of colour following after them like archaic birds.

Looking up I could see paper-like lanterns hanging from the sides of the buildings; all red, blue and purple, bobbing and swinging in the gentle breeze. Will pushed me on, further down the street, leaving the music and dancers to the delights of the locals. Slowly the lanterns got further and farther between, until nothing was left of the vibrant colours, wonderful, spicy-yet-sweet smells and beautiful people. We took another side alley at a jog and came out at a bustling London street. There were barrows full of produce, baskets of goods and men carrying great bundles of papers. This was the London I knew; the dull colours, the men and women barging past as they went about their daily duties.

"Right," Will said, looking perplexed while mirroring my smile. "Can we now get out of these clothes and find out where in hell we are!"

"Okay, are you alright?" I asked.

"What do you think?" he invited, rubbing his forehead with his fingers. "Look at us. Look at where we are. What are we doing here?" he cried.

"It could be worse, we could still be in the workhouse," I tried to reason.

"Let's just get some clothes and get out of here," Will huffed. Turning with an exasperated sigh he stalked up the street while raising a hand to indicate that we were to stay where we were.

I watched Will as he walked to where a huge shire horse was laboriously pulling an enormous cart stacked high with barrels of beer. He turned back, again indicating with a cautious hand for us to stay where we were. Will pressed his back against the wall of a shop before darting out. Crouched under the cart, he used it as a scouting point. As it trundled past a clothing stall I saw Will's arm dart out between the two large wooden wheels, grab a few garments and disappear. I did not see him resurface from beneath the cart as it rolled around a corner and out of sight.

Mary and I stayed put. We dared not move for fear that Will would not be able to find us. Our trepidation mounted as the minutes ticked by. Images ran through my head of Will being caught as a thief, getting his leg trapped by the cart, lying in agony on the ground. I reached over and took Mary's hand, our eyes never leaving the street in our desperate vigil. I had just opened my mouth to say we should go and look for him when his voice echoed from behind us.

"You girls looking for someone?"

We span around and were greeted with his cheeky, if all be it restrained, grin. Held aloft in his hands were new clothes. We ran over to him, grabbing at them as we laughed.

"Ask nicely," he sniggered, finally recouping some of his old humour.

I took my chance and tickled him under his arms. His defences dropped, he collapsed to the ground, his knees buckling immediately.

"That polite enough for you?" I joked, giggling as I helped myself to the haul. He had stolen a white shirt and grey trousers for each of us.

"Sorry, not much choice," he said, pushing himself up as he looked at the garments.

"They'll do," I said as I pulled the shirt over my head before shimmying out of my workhouse dress and dragging on the trousers.

They were both too big so I tucked in the shirt and rolled up the trousers, leaving our workhouse cloths in a pile for some scavenging child.

"Let's avoid that stall and go the other way," I suggested, peeking into the street once more.

We made our way to the end of the alley and turned right, heading down the main street. We walked through the mini metropolis, taking in our surroundings. Moving through the lively street I could not decide where to look, my attention being taken in so many different directions. Dominating a lot of the windows were posters. I struggled to read the words written in the odd script, looping and curling their way around strange images. I looked more carefully at the pictures. The more I studied them the odder they became. One had a drawing of a woman with a beard, another with miniature people. Larger than all of these however was the picture of a man. He looked grotesque, with his lumpy face, swollen lips and his head completely the wrong shape. People on the streets were pointing at the picture; they looked excited rather than horrified. Will took my hand and dragged me down the street, away from the disturbing posters.

I watched a lady parade past me selling sweet treats, my eyes following the wonderful delights before my attention was caught by the domineering presence of a large black man dressed impeccably in a grey suit. As I brushed past him I looked up and was transfixed by his eyes; the whites so bright in contrast to his dark skin and jet black irises. I jumped back in shock as he gave me a brief smile before walking on.

It was getting late, the stalls shutting down for the night, everyone concluding their business before nightfall. My stomach was beginning to protest at the lack of food. The smell of fresh bread wafting through the street made my mouth water, my hunger pangs increased in their insistence.

Eventually the bakery came into view. The shop was just closing when we came level with it. The owner jangled a large set of keys as he locked the door, gave it a shove and pulled at the handle before turning to leave.

So as not to arouse suspicion we wandered past, keeping our eyes averted. Once the man was gone we doubled back and came to a halt at the front door; behind which we knew awaited food. I looked around the building, assessing its facets. I spied a small, high set window at the back of the shop. It looked like the best way in but it would be tight.

"Mary, you think you can fit through that?" I asked, eyeing it eagerly.

"I, I don't know," she stammered, backing away from the bakery.

"You'll be fine," Will encouraged, "the bloke's gone, it's easy food."

"No, I know that, I'm just not sure." Mary was making fretful glances to us and then the window. She was biting her lip, wringing her hands nervously. "I can always try."

It was obvious she was not keen. I tried to hold back my irritated sigh as I came to terms with the fact that we would not be eating tonight. I looked again at the high window, trying to judge the height and width. It was clear Will would never fit, although thin from the workhouses meagre portions he had broad, muscular shoulders from his endless days of stone breaking. Looking down at myself I smoothed my hands over my hips, I would never fit.

I was about to suggest we try somewhere else when Mary eyed the wall with speculation. "I'll give it a go," she said, scrutinising the height of the wall, head cocked to one side, eyes narrowed. "Will, you'll need to give me a leg up."

I looked to Will with a raised brow.

"That's my girl, come on then, up you get," he said while positioning himself under the window upon bended knee. She looked determined as she took a small run up to the wall. Putting one foot on Will's knee, the other against the wall she could just reach the window-sill. Will took her foot and lifted her higher.

With one hard shove the window opened. It was lucky Mary was so small, the gap was tighter than it looked from the street; her slight body only just managing to squeeze through. Slowly she shuffled herself through the opening until her weight took over and she fell, head first through the window, landing with a thump on the other side.

"Mary?" Will tapped on the wall, "you alright…Mary?"

"I'm fine," she shouted, "what do you want?"

"I don't know. Get what's nearest and get out!" he called back.

For a few minutes we heard nothing, then a loud grinding noise.

"What in God's name are you doing?" Will cried, panicked by the noise.

"It's too high. I need to stand on something to reach the window," she called back breathlessly.

"What? If you move anything they'll know we stole stuff!"

"With the amount of bread missing they'll know anyway! You ready to catch?"

Bread began appearing through the window. She had stolen a whole loaf for each of us. I bundled them under my arms as Will kept a lookout.

"Ready to catch me?" she asked, her voice becoming clearer as she climbed closer to the window.

"Ready when you are."

With that I saw her triumphant face appear through the small frame.

"Don't come head first, what are you thinking? Come feet first so I can catch you!" Will scolded.

"I can't reach; you'll just have to try and catch me," she said, still persisting with her endeavour.

She was just easing her hips through the window when, with a small cry, she lost her grip and fell. Thankfully she avoided any substantial injury, using Will to break her fall. They were a mass of tangled limbs on the ground. Mary was the first to her feet with Will soon to follow, looking a little worse for wear.

"You elbowed me in my eye," he said, holding his hand over the affected eye, tears streaming from the other.

"It wasn't my idea to go up there. Got the bread didn't I?" she stated, her hands on her hips, a new defiant look in her eye.

"Yeah you did; sorry. And thank you," he apologised.

"Good job Mary," I said, giving her a brief squeeze.

She smiled back at me before walking away, putting a small skip in every other step.

"Where we going?" I asked, looking between Will and Mary's disappearing form.

"Back to the dock yard I guess," Will surmised with a shrug of his shoulders, before jogging to catch up with Mary. "Might be worth going around that strange place though; maybe find a place a bit further up river. I want to get as far away from that workhouse as possible," he continued, waving his arm in the general direction of Chinatown and the Workhouse.

Slinking back to the dock yard we followed the river upstream, picking our way through the deserting streets. Finally we reached St. Katherine Docks. It was a vast area full of imposing buildings and tall ships with billowing sails and creaking wood. We sat on one of the wooden walkways overhanging the water, swinging our feet as we ate our bounty.

"This'll be perfect," Will said as he chewed his food thoughtfully. "We'll be able to find work here, and if not, there are plenty of boats that can take us somewhere that will have work."

Both Mary and I stayed silent, I had no idea what kind of work we could get here, I had never worked at a dock yard before and I was fairly sure Will had not either. As the silence stretched between us Will endeavoured to fill the void. "Just think what we would be doing now. I would probably have had a year's worth of lashings in one go, you girls probably wouldn't be any better off and none of us would be eating for at least two days."

"You've sure changed your tune since this morning." I could not hold back the retort even though I knew it was not a fair one, Will had saved us from a terrible fate.

Will was silent for a moment, his handful of bread suspended in mid-air before his mouth. "I know, and I'm sorry, I, I didn't mean to kill him…"

"Don't," I stopped him, I could not relive that moment. "It wasn't right for me to say that. You're a good man Will." I reached over and took his hand, rubbing my fingers over the hard calluses that had formed on his palm.

"Come on, let's find somewhere warm for the night," Will eventually ventured into the retrospective silence, pulling us to our feet.

We bedded down for the night in an alcove at the back door to a brewery. With Will and Mary lying next to me I fell into a light sleep.

I was woken every so often by the sound of people shouting or a cart trundling past. I enjoyed watching the world go by in these insular moments. I found this new place exciting, it was so different from the part of London I had left. It was like we had travelled through that tunnel to a whole new land. I left my old life when I left that tunnel. This was a new beginning for all of us.

I watched as the day dawned warm and dewy. The light shimmering off the surface of the water made it look like liquid gems had formed over its surface. I sat and watched as jewels turned from sapphires to rubies and eventually into flakes of gold as the sun climbed higher in the sky. All too soon Mary and Will stirred from the depths of their dreams.

The activity around the Thames rose with the sun, people were walking briskly in every direction, going about their morning duties. In the distance I could see a group of children foraging along the river banks. They were paddling in the low waters and deep muddy banks. I watched as they collected trinkets from the dirt as they went.

"What are they doing?" I asked.

"Mudlarks." Mary stated as if it were obvious. I looked at her quizzically as she elaborated. "It's a job. My family and I used to do it before…before everything." I noticed her hesitation but did not comment. She continued as if nothing had happened. "You search the banks when the tide is low for anything you can sell. With all the factories and shops here I should think you can live quite well."

"What we waiting for then?" Will said jumping up, his interest immediately piqued.

He started scouring the shore line, leaping and pointing every time he thought he found something sellable. I eyed him dubiously but followed Mary's lead as she began to search with him. I was not convinced at first but soon saw that it could be a good way to scrape a living. Our hoard of goods was quickly growing.

As the weeks rolled by we relished our new freedom. The hours were long but we worked and ate as we needed. Virtually everything we found had some form of monetary value. Old cigarette butts could be sold back to the factory to be reused. Dog waste sold to the leather workers which they used to treat their products; shards of glass, rope, rags; all sellable. We did not have a lot between us but for the first time in all our lives we were free from the restraints society had placed upon us.

We kept to our alcove during the night, perfectly poised to search the shores before any of the competing mudlarks. We also got to know the workers from the local businesses. We soon worked out who would give us the best prices for our treasures and which establishments were to be avoided.

Not long after we had arrived we began to feel friction from the other street kids. Unbeknown to us the area was run by territories. Each group of mudlarks that occupied an area had to earn their patch. Our arrival had upset an easily disturbed balance.

The animosity crept in slowly, like a poisonous fog the hostility was subtle at first but building in its intensity as time ticked by. It started with the gangs just staring at us as we went about our daily business. They would watch us from the river banks, the larger lads flexing their arms in threat.

When we did not respond to these warnings they upped their game. We came back one day to find our carefully acquired items strewn across the mud. Any true treasures we had found; intact pieces of jewellery or almost complete garments of clothing had been damaged beyond repair, left stamped into the mud. This was not petty theft, this was a vendetta. This was their territory and we were an unwelcome intrusion.

It was as I was trying to piece together a brooch they had smashed that I looked up to see one of the gangs casually strolling past. It was the smirk on the leaders face at my futile attempts to repair it that made Will bite.

"You see something funny here do you? Well, do you?" he shouted at the gang.

The smirking youth laughed out loud, nudging his friends to follow his lead. "You'd better leave now," he called with a look of mock concern, "or else," he finished with a taunting smile.

"Or else what?" Will shouted back, showing no sign of intimidation.

Mary shrunk back while I stood solidly at Will's side and the gang walked on, the leader kicking a clump of mud at us as he passed.

We were enduring another attack one day, our goods lost to the river we had rescued them from, when Will finally had enough. He went to confront one of the gangs. Pulling himself up to his full height he marched over to them, he was like a dog ready for a fight. He did not look back as he continued down the narrow cobbled path. His shadow flickered as he walked through the shade of the buildings before being bathed in bright sun light once more. As the light hit the side of his face I could see the stark outline of his tensed jaw, the pucker of his furrowed brow. He had no intention of backing down.

I could not hear what was being said but I could see some of the boys getting animated, throwing their arms in the air and fronting up to him. As quick as a flash Will's arm had lifted and struck the leader of the gang square in the face. I saw him reel back, his hand moving to his nose as blood spilled over his lips. For one sickening moment I thought they were going to attack. Images of Will being beaten flashed unbidden to my mind, but Will had judged the situation well and the gang slowly backed off, not trusting to turn their backs on him until out of range of another attack.

After this Will got into a few more fights with other street gangs but it soon settled down. Luckily news travels fast through the streets and with each victory he earned more respect. By the end of autumn we had earned our own small territory: from the glass factory down to the far end of the dock yard. After many fights, confrontations and back-stabbings we finally had enough respect to be left alone.

Chapter 9

It was mid-autumn, the nights chill hanging in the air as a heavy fog encroached on our alcove. Huddled together for warmth we were sleeping peacefully, my head on Will's chest, my arm draped over his hips as he held me in place with his arms. Mary was beside us, her back pressed against Wills side for warmth. Suddenly we were roused from the depths of our dreams as an agonised scream cut through the air.

I awoke with a jolt as fire pulsed through my veins. As the noise dissipated my beating heart began to slow, the burnt-out fire leaving my body humming with unused energy. Before I had a chance to recover another shriek rang through the icy air, this time followed by high-pitched shouts for help that were quickly hushed.

Will was already on his feet; Mary and I quick to follow him out of the alcove. Together we crept through the darkness, guided only by the shouts of pain. It was as Will was peering around the corner, checking that the coast was clear, that the thought struck me: How strange that no one else seemed to be coming to this person's aid. Did the local occupants know something we did not? I took Mary by the hand and crept behind Will. We followed the agonising moans down an alley, stopping by a door stood ajar. I could hear great heaving sobs followed by a girl's pleading cries.

Another scream raked the air. I pulled myself into Will's arms, pressing my face to his chest. He held me to his side, his arm wrapped around my waist. I could feel the tension building in his body, his breath coming in hard gasps as he struggled with his indecision.

I looked up and saw the resolution settle in his eyes. He pressed his lips to my forehead before gently pushing me away. Will pushed the door open and stepped confidently over the threshold.

A grizzly scene met our eyes.

I stood transfixed, absorbing the disturbing scene unfolding before us. A girl was lying on her back, her simple dress pulled up, exposing a pair of porcelain legs smeared in red. She was being held on a bare wooden table by men in white aprons as she withered in a thick pool of blood. I watched as the crimson liquid dripped off the edge of the table, the floor holding a growing sticky pool. A woman was supporting her head, a rag pressed gently to her mouth. Another man was lurking in the background. He darted forward and started throwing rags on the floor in an attempt to mop-up the blood.

"Stop!" I cried in a choked, broken voice.

Will barged past me. "Stop what you're doing!" he growled, advancing into the room.

"I can't stop now you fool!" a balding man shouted from the bottom of the table, the girl's feet protruding under his arms at odd angles.

He uttered a word of unheard encouragement to the girl before twisting his arm with a quick jerk of his elbow. All of a sudden another torrent of blood was released from beneath her skirt. I heard the man utter a short prayer to God under his breath.

The girl had stopped protesting, her movements now feeble flinches of pain.

The man withdrew his bloodied hands. "I'm sorry."

I looked back to the girl to see her chest had stopped its rise and fall, her arms hanging limply from the edge of the table. In the back of my mind I noted Mary's quiet sobs.

"What happened?" Will asked; his voice barely above a whisper.

"An abortion gone bad," the man stated bluntly. "I am sorry," he muttered, turning his attention to the woman who we still cradling the girls head.

My eyes reluctantly slid to the woman as she tried to restore the girl's dignity. She collapsed with grief. I walked over to her, leaving Will to continue his interrogation. Taking a clean rag off the pile I dipped it into a bucket of water in the corner and began helping the woman clean her body.

"Who was she?" I asked, looking at her young face; she was no more than a child.

"She is my daughter." The woman's voice broke on the last word as she pulled a lock of tangled hair from her sweat dampened face, tucking it behind her daughter's ear.

"How," I took a breath before completing my question, "how did this happen?"

As she spoke I kept one ear trained on Will while trying to be sympathetic to the girl's mother. I was aware of raised voices coming from Will and the other men. This was shortly followed by the door closing sharply. I turned back to the mother who was lost in grief.

"It wasn't supposed to end like this," the woman sobbed, "she was attacked." Slowly, gently, she wiped away her daughter's drying tears. "Then we began to see what was growing inside her. It was a demon, borne of the attack," she spat bitterly; her face a mask of devastation and loss, her teeth gritted in anger towards the monster that had done this.

"She is at peace now," I whispered as I folded her daughter's hands across her swollen stomach.

As we washed her Mary edged closer and slowly she began to help. I saw her looking at the body wide eyed as she passed us clean rags. She never dared to touch the body. As we were finishing our ministrations I felt Will rub my arm with the back of his hand. I looked over my shoulder to see his eyes averted in respect.

"I'll go fetch a sheet," he uttered.

I nodded and watched as he left the room.

When he returned I was surprised to see him accompanied by the two men who had been restraining her. I looked at Will who, with the slightest movement of his head, told me to keep quiet. Forcing my attention back to the mother, I helped her wrap her daughter in the sheet Will had brought us.

When we stood back the men came forwards to collect her body. One of the men bent down and gently gathered her in his arms. Carrying her out he gave us a bob of his head in thanks. Her mother followed, supported by the other man, stumbling at the door before disappearing into the night.

"We can't leave it like this," I said picking up the dirtied rags and tossing them into a corner.

"I know," Will replied, "what a waste of a life." He sloshed the remaining water over the table and started wiping it down.

We did not finish until the early hours of the morning, leaving the room as the sun's morning rays shone through the open door, illuminating the blood-stained table.

"Leave the door open, so the spirit may pass," Mary asked as we left. She looked back into the room, almost longingly.

I stilled my hand on the handle, before gently pushing the door back. The light streamed into the room, bathing it in glorious light once more.

"That's what I would want, if I was her," Mary commented, still staring into the room, her brow furrowed in some unnameable emotion. I watched as she tilted her head to the side. "Almost beautiful, isn't it," she said, pointing to the dark red stain on the table. "Almost predictive, don't you think?"

"No, I don't think Mary," I said, trying to quell my feeling of unease at her strange words. I took her by the shoulders and steered her out into the ally. I took one last look at the room, at the way the light hit the desecrated table, at the eddies of dust as each tiny piece caught the light. Before I could give the subject any more thought I closed the door, giving Mary a small nudge as she opened her mouth to protest.

"Why did they do that to her?" Mary asked, obviously deciding not to challenge me as we started making our way back to our alcove.

"She was with child, a child she did not want," I explained, looking into her innocent eyes.

"But why kill her like that?" Mary pushed, childlike in her persistence to answer an unanswerable question.

"It wasn't their intention to kill her," Will clarified, "just the baby inside her. It just went wrong is all." He looked devastated. "I would never let that happen to either of you. Waste of a life if you ask me, of two for that matter," he finished sombrely.

I left the scene with a troubled mind, not only due to what we had just witnessed, but because of Mary's behaviour towards the event. The further we pulled her away from the routine and rigor of the workhouse, the worse she was becoming. Her strange changes in mood, the way she looked at things, it was beginning to trouble me.

I bedded down early that evening, conscious of my empty stomach and heavy heart. Will lay next to me, pulling me against him. I shuffled back, my body fitting perfectly against his. Mary chose to sleep away from us, settling herself deep in the corner of the alcove. All I could see was her eyes as they caught the sparks of the dying fire.

That night I lay awake, praying for the girl's soul. I did not blame the girl's mother, she was only doing what she thought was right. The pain she would feel for the rest of her life would be punishment enough.

As time went on the horrors of that night drifted into dark memory; some nights I would still awake with the image of her limp body burning behind my eyes. If it was not her waiting to haunt my dreams it would be my mother, my sister or my body, lying cold and prone, in her place. Will would look at me and know I had fallen back to that bloodied room. He would pull me closer to him, encasing me within his safe, solid soul.

"I would never let that happen to you," he would whisper, pressing his lips to my forehead.

Every so often we would hear the screams from that god-forsaken room and know pregnant woman was putting her life in another's hands. We did not answer the pleas, we knew what we would find, we knew there was no hope for those lost souls.

I was drifting in and out of sleep. It had been a long day and my mind was still reeling. It was as I was finally sinking into my world of dreams that I heard it.

A desperate scream cut through the air.

I began saying my prayer for the woman when I heard something I was not expecting. There was a shout, a strangled choke, a deep voiced cry for help.

Silence.

Chapter 10

I looked at Will, who had also been jerked awake at the sound of the first scream. Looking into my eyes he saw the thoughts tumbling through my mind.

"This is a bad idea," he reasoned.

"But something's going on."

"Yeah, I know, but we've been here before, this never ends well."

Will was trying to placate me but it was too late; I had made up my mind. It was different this time, I could feel it.

As I stumbled out of the alcove Mary began to stir. "What's going on?"

I did not reply, but held up my hand to silence her as she lurched towards me. "It's happening again," she sobbed.

"Shhh, I'm trying to listen," I said, trying to quell her murmurings.

"No, no, no," Mary cried, pressing her hands to her ears and shaking her head like a small child. "I don't want to hear it." I heard her choked sob as she pressed her head against my arm.

"No, you don't understand. I heard someone else. It sounded like a man."

"You know who will be there, come on, there is nothing we can do," Will said as he eased his hand around my waist, trying to coax me back into the alcove.

"But what if there is, what if she's not alone, or, or doesn't want to lose the baby? No Mary!" I rebuked as she tried to drag me back with Will. "I'm going to see what's going on. Are either of you coming with me?"

I could feel Wills eyes boring into me. Finally his dark silhouette stepped into the moon light. "You can stay if you like Mary. Actually, it may be better if you did."

The words had barely passed his lips when I heard her shuffle towards us.

"Wait, I need my…" Mary was cut short as another cry echoed across the still waters of the Thames.

"You don't need anything Mary," I snapped, no longer willing to wait while she dithered.

We stepped cautiously into the night; the new moon that gave us enough light to see by, meant we, in turn, could be seen. Its light glow reflected off the surface of the water as we made our way along the docks. We crept across the wooden boards, skirting between the tall wooden ships with their vast sails and the new metal vessels with their unforgiving sides and grinding poise. They sat in command of the rowing boats and dinghies where they bobbed in the water at the mercy of such unforgiving monstrosities. As the agonised calls continued we quickened our pace. I found myself losing my footing amongst the mooring ropes, the tight abrasive cords scraping at my skin as the slimy seaweed caused me to slip further. The docks yawned and groaned as the metropolis of boats breathed a life of their own in the tranquil water.

Finally, we made it to the alley. Stepping from the splintered wooden docks onto the hard cobbled street I heard a crash and a cry of pain.

"Hear that. I told you something was wrong."

"For once Clara, I'm in agreement with you." Will took my hand and pulled me towards the alleyway. We rounded the corner at a jog while Mary lingered, terrified, behind us. Stopping at the door we tried to listen. I heard a deep growl of anger, a high pitched squeal and an enraged scream as a fight broke out. The vicious calls shook the rafters as the chaos continued. With a shout of indignation from Will I pushed open the door.

The door swung open, bouncing back off its hinges. In the middle of the room stood a young woman, braced and ready to attack on the blood stained table. Her lips thinned as she bared her teeth, shrieking in a foreign language, her eyes wild with uncontainable rage. Held torturously in one hand was a bloodied knitting needle. Her other was laid protectively over her stomach. Her black maid's uniform hung off her in tatters, the white trim stained with blood.

Before I could take stock of the situation two men burst through the wall. The thin rotten wood cracked and splintered, sending blinding shards in every direction. As the room filled with shattered wood I brought my arm up to my face, desperately trying to protect my eyes and mouth. The room quieted as the wood, dust and mould took effect. The men were subdued by the unbreathable air; the grunts and scuffles of the fight turning into hacking coughs.

As the dust settled I lowered my arm. One of the men was hunched, forced into a head lock, his crisp black suit torn and covered in dirt. I recognised the one holding him as one of the men from when we were here last. This time, instead of helping a grieving mother out the door he was trying to force this obviously upper-class gentleman uncouthly out of the way. Unfortunately he was losing his grip. With an almighty wrench his arm gave way and he emitted a scream of his own. Cradling his arm he ran for the door, pushing me into the frame and he lurched past.

It was not until then that I saw the small balding man on the floor, I recognised him from last time too. He now lay flat on his back, his eyes staring blankly at the dusty cobwebs above. I could see a growing patch of blood spreading from beneath his body. My eyes travelled to the table where the woman stood, clutching the dripping needle in a desperate hand

The man in the suit covered in debris from the demolished wall stepped up to us.

"What are you doing here?" he snarled.

None of us answered.

Will stumbled further into the rasping silence. As I continued to stare at the woman on the table Will pushed deeper into the room. He sunk to his knees beside the balding man and inspected him, lifting a limp hand, leaning down to try and feel his breath on his cheek. "He's dead," he finally stated, looking up at the woman. "She killed him," he said, turning his wide eyes back to the well-dressed man.

"It's not her fault," he murmured quickly as fear ripped across his face. "You have to understand," he begged, taking a step towards Will.

"It's alright, we do understand. We heard you, we came here to help," I said as I stepped forward. "What do you need?"

"Food, be good, please," the woman answered in broken English.

The man looked back at her and spoke in a strange language. She nodded her head to his mystery question. He walked up to her and held out his hands. She bent down and gently placed the needle on the table. Taking his outstretched hands she finally climbed off the table. He wrapped his arm around her waist as they cautiously approached us.

"We don't have a lot, but what we do have we will be happy to share," I offered.

Will glared at my imprudent words

"Thank you for your kind offer, but we couldn't, it wouldn't be right." As he went to lead his woman away he stopped. He was looking at Mary. I saw him follow her gaze back to the bloodied maid and lung at her. He caught her as she fell, cradling her to the floor.

"What's wrong with her," he asked, panic dominating his tone as he picked her up and held her close. Her head lolled back, hanging at an odd angle. "She's, she's not. No, she can't be," he cried, jostling her with his arm.

"She's still breathing," Will said stepping close, "she's just had enough for now. Look, she's exhausted; you look a mess, come back, have some food, get some sleep and then see how you feel in the morning," he continued, the undertone of reservation clear in his tone.

The man looked like he was about to decline when I stepped in.

"How far are you going to get with her in that state?" I asked, pointing to the woman hanging prone in his arms.

Eventually he nodded. "What about him?" he asked, pointing with his chin to the body on the floor.

"Let's just keep it to, you were never here, we were never here and if anyone asks, we met three streets away," Will said, already ushering them towards the door. "Just follow Mary," he added, pointing to where she was pressed against the door frame, her fearful eyes sweeping to the floor as all eyes turned to her.

"It's alright Mary, they need our help," I said as I walked over to her and took her hand. "Follow us," I reiterated as I led Mary out the door.

Will walked behind us, closing the door softly behind him before scooting past and falling into step beside me.

"I don't like it," Mary whispered past me, her comment aimed at Will.

"I know, but Clara's right, we can't leave them."

Mary nodded once but stayed mute.

The stranger followed us back to our alcove, careful to keep his distance. I could hear him whispering a lament of love to the woman as he walked, clutching her close to his chest.

As we rounded the final corner to our alcove I turned back to wave him forwards.

"Please come, sit," I said, gesturing to the floor, "we'll get a fire on the go and you'll soon warm up."

I led by example, sitting myself crossed legged by our pile of wood while Will took out our precious piece of flint and his knife. Mary sat next to me, staring dolefully at Will.

Still holding the woman close to his chest he chose to sit away from us, his exit clearly visible. As he sat Will attempted to light the fire. The spark refused to take. Somehow the tinder had become damp overnight, more than likely due to our few hours of neglect. As the minutes ticked by the woman began to mutter and moan, her head roving slightly as she tried to wake. With his whispered encouragement she quietened once more, her head resting on his chest. Again, with a groan of frustration Will scraped the flint with the knife and finally the bright, white spark landed on the kindling and glowed orange as it consumed a dry piece of moss. With practiced skill and care it did not take long for the embers to turn into a blazing fire. I crawled to the back of the alcove to retrieve the bread I had bought yesterday.

"It's better if you warm it by the fire first," Will pointed out as he stuck his roll on a stick, holding it above the flames to warm through.

The man looked at us warily before taking the two pieces I offered him. Will gave me a nervous toss of the head; it was obvious I was the one appointed to doing the digging. I cleared my throat.

"I'm Clara; this is Will and our friend Mary."

Will gave them a cheery wave from his speared bread while Mary gave them a quick glance before returning to her meal.

"You're safe here, whatever happened, this is the one place they won't come looking, no one ever comes looking here," I finished with a grateful smile, thinking back to Will's encounter with the marshal. No one had ever come asking questions and a wanted poster had never been published.

"Thank you," he said with a small inclination of his head, but he offered nothing more.

As the silence enveloped us Mary made her way to the back of the alcove where she curled herself into her customary tight ball. Will looked to me and I nodded. "We're going to turn in, just make yourself comfortable."

"If I were you I'd come a little further in, they won't appreciate you lying in the middle of the road when they try and load the boats come morning," Will interjected helpfully.

"Good night." I smiled awkwardly as I stood to walk to the back of the alcove with Will.

"I don't want them here," Mary whispered as Will and I lay down.

"Enough Mary," I sighed.

"Go easy," Will muttered, "and go to sleep Mary."

As Will drifted off to sleep I stayed awake, watching as the man gazed endlessly at the woman, his gentle eyes illuminated by the quietly flickering fire.

Slowly, as the embers burnt low and Will's breathing slowed, the man started to relax.

"What happened to the two of you?" I whispered into the silence, my voice sounding haunting in the eerie stillness of night. "How did you end up here?"

The man looked to me, surprised.

"I thought you were sleeping," he said, his eyes returning to the woman.

I stayed in Wills arm; my absence was more likely to wake him than my voice. "What happened?"

He took a deep breath, measuring my integrity, considering how much I was to be trusted. Eventually he spoke. "My name is Matthew and this is Natalia." He flourished his hands elegantly as he introduced himself and the woman, his ingrained training in etiquettes taking over. "I am Lord Alfred's Nephew," he said pointing vaguely behind us. "Natalia was one of the cleaning maids, she is from France. It was not supposed to happen like this, we were safe, careful. Well, not careful enough," he noted, drawing attention to her obvious condition. "When my uncle found out, he said he would handle it. Before I had a chance to question anyone on the matter they had taken her. I managed to pay off one of the servants to tell me where they had gone. I followed. I could not leave her, you must understand this. No matter what they said, what they did, it did not matter."

"But it mattered to your Uncle."

"Yes, very much so," Matthew replied, taking his lover's hand.

"So what's your plan now?"

"Find passage on one of the merchant ships. I have family in France, as does Natalia; who hopefully have not heard of our indiscretion. We will marry and make a new start," he said with vehemence, as if daring me to argue.

"We know most of the merchants, I'm sure we could find a ship that will take you," I offered, ignoring his challenging tone.

"That would be, most kind of you." He looked taken aback by my generosity. He opened his mouth to say more but looked away. I saw his throat move and the muscles in his chest contract; he took a deep breath as he looked into the darkness.

"Thank you, Clara," he said eventually, looking back at me with the ghost of a smile.

Early the next morning Will went to put the word out while Natalia rested in the alcove. Matthew and I decided to work our way through the shops, getting supplies together that would see the two of them, and potentially a new baby, through the voyage. It did not take long for me to warm to Matthew. He was a kind man and, despite our first impressions, he had a gentle soul.

"I don't know how we could ever reciprocate for all you have done for us," he muttered as we browsed the shelves, looking for warmer clothes that would be necessary for the cold nights on board ship.

"What were we supposed to do?" I asked, looking up at him quizzically.

"What everybody else seems to do, nothing."

"Ah yes, but we are not everyone else," I smiled as I walked to the counter, my arms brimming with goods. "I know how it feels to be looked over, for people to do nothing, so does Will. We've been the ones doing nothing before," I admitted. "The way I see it, it's got to change some time, it's got to start with someone. Who knows, maybe one day you could do the same for someone else and then they will do the same again," I said with a hopeful smile as I dumped the effects on the counter, where I was distracted by the shop assistant.

"Would that be all Sir?" the assistant offered.

"Yes thank you," Matthew answered before turning back to me. "Your hope, it's moving," he said, looking at me compassionately as he fished out his purse.

I tried to be polite, keeping my eyes averted as he dug through his money bag but it was obvious by the size and amount of digging he had to do that it was full.

"Is that everything?" I asked as we left the shop.

"I think so; I would like to get back to Natalia."

"Yes, I'm not sure who was more upset by that arrangement, Natalia or Mary," I said with a laugh.

It did not take Matthew and me long to get back. We found Mary searching the shore line with Natalia sleeping peacefully in the shade. Matthew moved forwards to wake her.

"Leave her be," I said, holding him back with a hand. "It won't do her any harm to sleep a little longer."

"Maybe I'll just sit with her a while," he whispered.

I watched as he walked over to her. He crouched down and brushed a stray lock of hair from her face. As she stirred he lay down next to her, pulling her into his arms. I could not help the gentle smile that lifted my cheeks. I left them to their quiet world, leaving to help Mary search the shore line for any last minute finds.

By lunch Will returned with forged permits for passage, a dock number and the captain's name, but most importantly bearing fresh, still hot, pies. As he approached I saw Matthew lean over and whisper something in Natalia's ear. By the time we came level with them they were both sat up, looking expectant.

"Here," Will said handing out the pies, "and here are your papers. The ship leaves tonight."

"Thank you," Matthew said after swallowing his mouthful of food. "Are you sure it's all organised? He's expecting us?" he questioned, offering the papers back to Will.

"He'll see you right," Will answered, pressing the papers back into Matthew's hand. With a worried smile Matthew gently slid the papers into an inside pocket of his dirty jacket.

"How are you feeling Natalia?" I asked.

"I good. It is, it be…" she looked around us, trying to find the right words. Eventually she turned to Matthew and spoke to him in her own tongue, gesturing with her hands. He mumbled into her ear and she continued, "yes, here it beau, er, beautiful, but dark, very dark."

"You want to go back to France?" I asked.

"Yes, have family, friends, have all we need." She smiled as she took Matthew's hand. "We have all we need." She gave Matthew a reassuring nod.

When I first met them I saw Natalia as a helpless waif in need of rescue and Matthew as her saviour. Now I saw I had it the wrong way around. Natalia was the one saving him. I could see it in the way she held herself, her straight back, her head held high and her bright brown eyes.

"You're going to be fine Matthew," I said, trying to suppress my laugh. Natalia caught my eye and gave me a knowing smile.

We finished our meal, laughing at over-told stories and sharing old fables before helping Matthew and Natalia pack their new belongings. Matthew checked and re-checked every detail, going over everything with Will as Natalia and I sat on the bank, enjoying the last of the day's warm rays.

"Are you going to help him?" I asked Natalia.

"And spoil his, his…importance, he likes to think he cares for me," she said, her eyes dancing with humour. "This be good for him, he will learn. But maybe you right." With another smile she got slowly to her feet, stretching her back and arms as she stood. Together we wandered over to Will and Matthew.

"This is the first time you've done this sort of thing?" I asked as we came up to them.

"What, leave my family, friends, everything I've ever known? Yes."

"Don't worry; it'll get easier with time," Will offered with a smile.

We walked them to the dock. Matthew moved slowly, keeping Natalia under his arm, constantly checking behind him.

"This is you," Will said pointing to an old wooden ship, "the Captain's called Henri, he's a good man."

"Thank you," Matthew said with uncompromising sincerity. "We could never repay such a debt; I truly hope that one day we meet again. Please, take this. It is all we can give you; but it will never be enough for what you have done." He forced a small bag into my hand as Natalia kissed my cheek. They embraced Will and me briefly one last time before giving Mary a reassuring smile. Then they were gone.

I tipped the contents of the bag into Will's waiting hands; it was money, more money than I had ever held.

* * *

That money was our life line; it was the thing that kept us from drowning, the raft that kept us out of the worst of London's grim underworld. Unfortunately it is not something that lasts. Like the unrelenting tide that wears away land, like the battering wind that grinds stone and fells trees. All things, despite hard work, perseverance and good will come to an end.

My thoughts are invaded when a man pulls back the cloth door and leans through the doorway. "We're all set to sail."

"I just need a little longer."

"Too much longer and we'll miss the tide."

"Okay, I'll be right out."

As he leaves with an irritated sigh my eyes fall back to my leather bound volume. With renewed vigour I begin to scrawl across the page.

I have to finish my story. They have to know the truth.

Chapter 11

For three years we lived as mudlarks, using the money from Matthew and Natalia to help us live a little better. We were careful not to waste a single half penny, only dipping into our precious savings when we had nothing left to fall back on. The summers we would spend by the river, and when winter arrived we would find cheap accommodation, a room or cellar; anywhere we could escape the biting cold. What little we had was a constant battle to keep from the prying fingers of other mudlarks. Despite our work, savings and careful calculations our money was beginning to run out.

We were embarking on our third winter. The afternoons were turning dark with icy winds and thrashing rains that lasted for days, the freezing nights causing the banks of the Thames to become crystallised mud. We were desperately trying to find warmer accommodation to see us through the worst of the snow storms and frosts. Over the years we had gotten to know the area. Because of the docks the lodgings here were expensive and every winter the struggle got harder. Our savings had diminished and no matter how hard we worked we could not recover the money. We could not stay where we had previously; it had been taken under new ownership and the management were not as sympathetic as the former occupants.

So we wouldn't lose too much money looking for lodging only one of us would go on the hunt each day. Today was Mary's turn; Will and I staying back to work our area of the river.

I was in my own, currently dreary world, picking through the cold mud; the prospect of a winter with no shelter weighing heavily on my mind.

"Clara! Look what I've found!" Will, now tall and lean with broad shoulders, called from the knee deep mud, lifting me from my thoughts.

Looking up I saw a cheeky grin stretched across his face, his hair falling in disarray into his eyes. I knew that look far too well; obviously my gloomy thoughts had invaded his happy sphere and he was not going to stand for it.

"No!" I called back, crossing my arms across my chest as I gave him a knowing look.

"Why?" he asked innocently, as his eyebrows climbed in mock shock.

"We have both been here before. You say you've found something splendid causing me to rush to your side. When in actual fact you're bored and have a masterful plan full of mischief and mayhem," I answered succinctly.

"Maybe?"

His grin told me all I needed to know. He chortled to himself as he continued his search. I bent down, shaking my head in mock shame. I was considering another playful aside when a gleam of light caught my eye. I knelt down, turning my head to try and see the glint again. Finally I saw a flash. It was a fragment of glass that had caught the glare of the dwindling sun.

I carefully eased my fingers into the sludge and freed it from its muddy prison. It was a triangular shard of green glass with curved sides. I dug around the surrounding area and found more of the same. By the time I had finished excavating the area I had enough pieces to almost make an entire bottle. I collected the bits together and put them into the cloth bag Will had bought me the first year we arrived here. I had repaired it so many times it was made up of nothing but patches of mismatched material with heavy stitching from whatever yarn I could find at the time. I ran my fingers over the rough fabric, picking off the more offending pieces of dirt that had become stuck in its course weave.

Bringing myself out of my reverie I called to Will, "I'm going up to the Glass Factory, got quite a lot and should get a fair bit for it. You got anything for me to take up?"

"Na, nothing for the glass, most I've got is for the dye factory and I'll go by later with that."

He bowed extravagantly to me from the deep mud. I curtseyed back playfully, my boundless dirty-blond curls tumbling over my face as I dipped my head. I swung a handful of hair off of my face as I stood laughing, the curls falling down my back once more. I waved and started making my way to the factory. I had to pass the dye factory to sell the glass but the owner never showed me the same level of respect he showed Will. He would be guaranteed a better price than me.

I followed the Thames up river, taking my time to browse the stalls as I passed. I was looking at a carved, ivory fronted locket on display when I caught a glimpse of something that made me stop. As a man walked past I had seen the paper folded under his arm. I rushed on to the Newspaper stand and stared down at the front page. It was dominated by a drawing of a cloaked figure wielding a huge knife. Below him, quaking on the ground, was a woman. The artist had clearly drawn tears streaming down her face, her mouth hanging open in an unheard scream. The headline read, 'Ghastly Murder in the East End' with a caption below stating, 'Dreadful mutilation of a woman. Who will catch The Leather Apron?' It was printed in large black lettering. With a feeling of fear creeping over me I looked over my shoulder, half expecting to see the murderer stood behind me. The paperboy caught my eye, "You alright miss?"

"Yes, I'm fine thank you," I muttered, placing the paper carefully back onto his stall.

I hurried down the street, preoccupied by what I had read. Will and I had heard the stories but they had come to us through the street kids and we had assumed they had just been scaremongering; now however it seemed real and a lot closer to home.

It had started with rumours of people being stabbed and attacked, but it seemed like nothing, at least not compared to what used to go on back in Devils Acre. Then it became more than just hearsay, people said they knew the person who had been attacked, that the monster was targeting just women. The latest news was that parts of the woman had been taken away. Some said he took them as souvenirs, others for black magic. The most horrifying part was that no one knew what he looked like, how he spoke. He could have been walking behind me, tracking me, and I would have no way of knowing.

As my irrational mind got the better of me for a second time I looked behind. A group of women looked at me, obviously irritated that I had stopped in the middle of the street. I turned around and hastened my step, pulling my shawl a little tighter around my shoulders.

As I made my way to the Glass Factory I decided I would not mention the newspaper article to Will. After all, there was nothing we could do about it and bringing the article to his attention would just make him worry.

My spirits lifted when I eventually made it to the factory. I came here as often as I could; the people were kind and they gave us fair prices. I knocked on the side door and waited for a reply. Walter came to the door, his large belly preceding him as he peered around the door. As he saw me a light smile lifted his wild beard.

"Hello Clara, come on in," he called as he opened the door wider, gesturing for me to enter. "A profitable day for you I hope?"

"So far, so good. Hopefully it's about to get a little better," I said, raising an eyebrow at him as I sashayed past with a smile.

He led me through the familiar factory. Walking past the workers, each at their own station, I was mesmerized by their work, the beautiful vases, bottles, and glasses they made. I walked past Alfred's lean, sinewy form as he rolled a piece of red glass along a pole, turning it into a beautiful shape. I could see the look of deep concentration on his lined face as he worked. He turned the pole and adjusted the angle and the glass transformed. It was like the bulb of a flower on the brink of exploding into bloom. He angled it so that it opened more at one end, the first petal to emerge from its fragile cocoon. The skill it took to make such a piece was beyond me. I caught his eye and he gave me a swift wink, not daring to take his attention away from his unique work of art. I walked past the other employees, admiring their workmanship.

"Never miss a step you kids," Walter chortled to himself. I turned to see him watching me as I studied the men working. I scurried to catch up and we made our way deeper into the belly of the factory.

We stepped around a billow of hot steam that arose from the boiling water as a piece of glass was cooled. Walter pulled a handkerchief from his threadbare trousers and wiped it over his face where beads of sweat were working their way down his face. He finished by patting under his arms, wiping back of his neck and rubbing beneath his stained shirt. Mirroring his actions I wiped my face with the back of my arm; I could feel the tiny hairs beginning to stick to my head as the moisture and steam began to coat my skin like a suffocating blanket.

We eventually reached the office at the far end of the building. It was full of the usual clutter; stacks of paperwork piled high, subdued only by odd shaped pieces of glass. He shuffled the papers on the desk into a pile and stuffed them into a drawer. The only items left were a dip pen, ink pot, the official factory stamp and two sheets of paper.

"Let's see it then?"

I upturned my bag onto his desk, allowing my rescued treasure to fall from its confines. Walter fingered through the pieces, checking for any manufacturing marks. He found a large piece and picked it up to take a better look. Lifting it to the small window he allowed the light to pass through it.

"Looks like good quality stuff," he mumbled more to himself than to me while still staring up at the glass. He looked at me, gauging my reaction, "I can give you two half pennies for the lot."

"It's at least worth three! You said yourself it was good quality."

"It's not that good quality," he retorted with a dry smile.

"Alright, how about two half pennies and a farthing?" I grinned.

"Done!"

We shook hands. He knew I never accepted the first offer; it was now more of a joke than actual bartering.

He put the official glass factory stamp on the top of each piece of paper, dipped his dip pen into the inkwell and painstakingly wrote out two identical receipts, one for each of us. He took the money from his pocket as I wrote a scratchy, almost unrecognisable, C Forge on the bottom of each piece.

I left the factory with receipt and money in hand, now enjoying the cold breeze that was blowing off of the Thames, ridding my skin of the sticky residue that had built up in the heat of the factory.

I walked to the docks, waving at Will as he came into view. Wading towards me, his hands were full of unrecognizable objects.

"Could you lend me your bag? I can barely keep hold of all this!" he called from the mud.

I ran up to him, my ankles sinking deep into the thick silt. His hands were full of a mixture of broken fragments. Examining it more closely I saw it mostly contained cigarette butts.

"Let's get it to the bank first and separate it out."

I took a handful of the spoils and made my way to the top of the bank, laying it out on a plank from the ship yard. We meticulously sorted the items into small piles based on where they could be sold.

"It's getting late. We're not going to have time to sell all this tonight," Will mused, looking sullen at the prospect of lost money.

"Of course we will, you take half, I take half. We'll be done in a few hours."

"Sounds like a plan," he said, obviously trying to sound happier than he felt.

"What is the matter?" I sighed.

"Don't you think Mary should have been back by now?"

"Yes," I looked up the river, almost expecting her to come bounding down the river bank towards us, "but she probably had to go quite far to look for new places to stay. It's getting harder every year. You know Mary, she won't come back until she has somewhere for us," I tried to placate him, while inside my stomach was twisting with anxiety.

He huffed before reluctantly giving in, "alright; let's sell this stuff so we can get back before Mary." I saw his eyes mirror mine as they swept the banks looking for her. "I'll see you in a few hours." Collecting his half of the hoard he stood and gazed at me, a long searching look in his eye, before heading for the main street.

I made my way around the town, passing through my regular haunts. I had made a good profit; the tobacco factory had given me a good price, he must have been running low on stocks. My last stop was the fabric factory at the far end of the district. Thankfully I managed to sell all my remaining items; not for a lot, but it was better than nothing.

I had taken longer than expected and darkness had begun to creep in. The shops casting their sharp long shadows across the streets plunged my world into darkness while the sky remained dark blue above. I had no way of knowing where Mary was or if Will was back. The thought of them alone in the streets with the Leather Apron murderer on the prowl made the skin on the back of my neck prickle as the delicate hairs stood on end. A cold shiver ran down my back.

I ran back through the quietening streets, imaginary shadows chasing me down the alleyways as old nightmares came back to haunt me. Every shadow held the glimpse of a piercing blue eye, a dark movement within the gloom. Suddenly I felt like I was being dragged back to Devils Acre, could feel the callous call of those dark streets in the images conjured by the artists of the news. I got back to our alcove, dragging the air into my lungs, to find neither Will nor Mary waiting for me. I crossed my arms over my body and leant my back against the wall. The sky had turned dark and the streets become quiet before I heard footsteps. I recognised them immediately as Will's.

"No sign of Mary then?" he asked as he approached.

"Not yet."

"She shouldn't be long." Will sighed as he turned his face to the heavens. The skies darkened to pitch as a cloud rolled over the new moon. "It's not like her, she's only just started to go out on her own, she should have been back by now."

"Don't worry Will. She's been doing a lot better. She even spoke to Walter the other day."

"Yeah, that was a shock," he laughed.

"More than a shock, did you see Walter's face," I giggled.

Laughing at the memory Will walked towards me. Standing in the entrance of the alcove I could see his lean frame silhouetted against the moons bright glow.

He stopped a few paces away and buried his hands deep in his pockets; I could make out his mischievous eyes assessing me, a daring glint hidden behind his humour.

A smile lifted his cheeks as he playfully rolled his head forwards, looking up at me through his dark lashes. He walked lazily up to me, stopping inches from my body. Pulling his hands from his pockets he leant back, gently placing his hands on either side of my face before lowering them slowly, his hands coming to rest at my midriff. He ran his hands around my waist, settling them at the small of my back. Resting his chin on top of my head I felt him take a deep sigh. I snaked my hands around his hips and rubbed his back, trying to relieve some of the day's tension. I felt him rest more of his body weight against me as he lent his head into my hair.

I closed my eyes and rested my head against his chest. I smiled as I guessed where he had been. He had been to the leather factory; I could smell the familiar conditioner they used. His shirt held the hint of smoke; I guess I had not been the only one to frequent the glass factory today. He also smelt of sweat, indicative of a hard days labour, but above all else, he smelt of Will. I nuzzled the side of my face into his chest and closed my eyes. Instinctively I lifted my head. For the first time, our lips met. Fire rolled through my body at the intimate touch. I responded, kissing him, pushing away from the wall until my body was flush against his. I could feel his muscles tense and release beneath his shirt. Feel the slight shift in his weight. He took a sharp intake of breath as his hand ran up my back, nestling in my hair. He pressed his forehead to mine as our lips parted, our bodies still close, our breathing in time as he held me.

As we broke our embrace I looked up to see the stars twinkling above us in the vast expanse of heaven, their delicate rays blessing our long awaited union. I pressed my lips to his once more as darkness enveloped us, like the comforting arm of a long lost friend. We were united under the eternal beauty of the stars.

Suddenly a chillingly familiar scream racked the air. Will tore himself away from me and started towards the sound. In a single second my worst fears were confirmed. Mary was shouting for help, the distant echoes only now reaching my ears. In the moon light I saw her trip and fall, skidding on the dirty ground. Then I saw the shadows, emerging from the darkness like demons from a dark nightmare. A group of men were chasing her, hunting her like an animal, their laughter and jeering echoing indistinctly off the surface of the still water as we ran to her.

We sprinted to Mary. She was still on the floor. We skidded to a halt, barely keeping our footing on the filth strewn street. Will and I bent down and hauled her to her feet, but we were too late. They came upon us from all sides, surrounding us. They shoved Will. Trying to support himself he reached out and grabbed Mary and me. We fell, landing in a heap on the floor. The gang towered over us, ready to attack.

Will pushed himself to his feet and stood, his feet planted firmly, his body tensed in front of us. He was hit in the face and then the stomach. As he fell to his knees another dragged him to his feet and gave him an uppercut to his kidney. As he collapsed to his knees and doubled over in pain a third man grabbed him by the throat and dragged him away, his body lost.

Panic swelled inside me as I looked upon the men bearing down on us, my heart hammering against my chest. As fear purged my body of all thought and feeling my world slowed. All I could hear was my ragged breathing. Then I saw him and my world stopped. John was standing before us; his blue eyes alight and fevered in his bloodlust. A wave of horror hit me as I was transported back. Once more I was that small scared child staring into the eyes of evil. I could see his fingers twitching in anticipation, his head twisting and snaking as he closed his eyes, a look of divine pleasure on his face. His body was low and tense, glorying in our terror. Finally my hearing caught up with my other senses.

John was talking in a sickly sweet voice. "That's not the way to show your appreciation at our offer." He cocked his head to the side. "I told you the price, and I expect payment upfront." He leaned forward on the last word, inhaling Mary's fear, his eyes wide as he drank her in.

* * *

Even the memory of him causes bile to rise in the back of my throat, burning my mouth at the memory of the vile animal. I push the book away from myself angrily, wiping my hands down my dress as though I had been contaminated just by reliving that memory.

My violent outburst causes the book to hit the candelabra and as it wobbles precariously I lurch forward. The candle does not fall but I watch as a single drop of wax falls from the wick and settles on the parchment.

In a rush of unthinking haste I turn the page and press them together, effectively sealing the pages. If only it was that easy to rid myself of John in reality.

Chapter 12

A small whimper of terror escaped Mary's lips before they attacked. John reached his hand forward with easy, uncaring grace and caressed her head, his fingers sinking into her dark hair. She stared back at him, unmoving, her eyes locked with his as her lips trembled. He gazed at the fear etched into every line and tear streak of her terrified face, a sick smile playing across his lips. Grabbing a fistful of hair he jerked her head back. With one sneering glance back at me he dragged her away.

As she was hauled backwards her eyes met mine; they were wide with fear. "Help me," she screamed as she kicked and thrashed. I could see her body twisting as she grabbed at cracks in the buried cobbles. Finding no purchase on the grimy ground her fingers left deep gouges in the filth-ridden street. "Help!" she screamed, her pained wail cutting through me like an icy blade.

Before I could get to my feet I was struck across the face by an unseen fist. I felt a numbness spreading through my body. Dark spots began to cloud my vision. I felt another hit before my head struck rock with a crack that reverberated inside my head. My eyes flashed wide as adrenalin coursed through my veins. A sound like thundering water crashed past my ears, the world swimming in front of me.

Lost in a sea of fear I could see nothing but distorted shapes and veiled colours that seemed to loom from the darkness. Trying to get up I felt a great weight on top of me. I tried to drag air into my lungs but the force crushing my ribs stopped all movement. I pushed against the object, my hands coming into contact with a man's unrelenting chest. I could feel his ribs expanding and retracting faster and faster as his breathing quickened. His hands seized my wrists. My arms were pushed above my head, the grit from the street grinding painfully on the backs of my hands as the pressure increased.

In the pitch of night, with nothing but Mary's whimpering screams and this monsters laboured breathing in my ear, my fear finally engulfed me. Tears spilled from my eyes and mucid liquid defiled my face as he forced his lips to mine. I clenched my jaw closed, trying to rip my face away from his, until I ran out of breath. My lips parted and as he forced his mouth to mine. Once more I screamed. His panting breath was forced into my mouth, the foul smell of decay thick in the air. I turned my head, trying to take a clean breath, to rid myself of the vulgar stench. I needed air. I could feel myself slowly suffocating.

I shook my head, straining away from the pungent air engulfing my lungs, again trying to take a clean breath. The brute took my wrists in one calloused hand as he grabbed a handful of my hair with the other. He twisted his fist, pulling my hair tight. Forcing my head back he laughed as he saw the fear in my eyes, his angular, high cheek-boned face looking superior as he gazed down at me.

He had me pinned to the floor. Knowing I was at his mercy he pressed his face to mine harder, his coarse facial hair scratching my face. He was shifting his lower body, pushing my legs open, his breathing becoming ragged, his lips not leaving mine.

Seizing my only chance of escape I took his bottom lip in my teeth, biting until I tasted blood. He ripped himself away, roaring in pain. Releasing my hands he showered me with blows. I brought my arms down and covered my face, pulling my head to my chest as I tried to defend myself. Between the deluge of blows I looked up at him. In a single glimpse I saw the damage I had done. I had ripped away his bottom lip at one side, the lump of flesh hanging grotesquely from his face. He screamed in deranged anger as blood poured from the wound. He slowed his attack, kneeling over me, his breathing heavy.

He looked grim as he gazed upon me, his eyes narrowed and calculating. A dark shadow crept across his face, distorting his features. As he took a heaving breath I took my chance. I hit him in the mouth with all the strength I had left in me. As he reeled back I rolled over and crawled away from where he was gasping in pain.

"John! Aaron! Jones!" he screamed, his arms stretched back, his muscles tense, his chest heaving. His eyes were wild. Bloodied spit flew from his mouth as he hollered to his accomplices for help. He took a breath to shout again and I kicked him just above the stomach, silencing him with a grunt of pain. Finally he keeled over like a great falling tower. When he did not rise from my attack I looked up, surprised but grateful, to see small moving dots of lights coming from every direction. The commotion had alerted people to our cause. As people poured from the building overshadowing us the one that attacked me crawled away, forcing himself to his feet. He stumbled into the shadows of an alley and was gone.

As our rescuers closed in the three men who had Will made their escape, they were nothing but wraiths in the night. Will was on the floor, unmoving. I looked to Mary to find John nowhere in sight. Moments later we were encircled by concerned friends.

"I'm fine," I told Alfred, recognising his lean, wiry frame silhouetted against the glowing lanterns of our rescuers. I continued to push him away as he tried to check me over. "No really, I'm fine. Will and Mary, please, are they okay?" I asked, gesturing towards my family.

I walked over to Mary, afraid of what I was going to see. Maude, Alfred's wife, was fussing over her, giving whispered instructions to idle bystanders. She looked willowy and delicate as she knelt over Mary; her waves of long silver hair fell like a veil, obscuring her face. I knelt down beside Mary and squeezed her hand. She looked through me, her eyes staring blindly into the night as she retreated into herself.

"Someone fetch a blanket, there should be some by the furnace in the factory," Maude ordered gently.

I was taken aback by the calm aura she shrouded us in. While we waited she took the shawl from her back and laid it over Mary as she tried to sooth her with gentle whispers.

I could do nothing but stand in shock. Eventually Alfred's out of breath voice broke the descending silence.

"Here, will this do?" Alfred asked. Without looking up Maude extended her hand for the blanket and draped it over Mary. "Walter said they can come back to the factory," he continued.

"Yes, yes," Maude muttered, her eyes not leaving Mary. "Take her up, we'll follow," she said, stepping back.

Alfred bent down and picked her up, cradling her close to his chest. "Hush, hush, easy girl, I've got you," he murmured softly to her as he turned towards the factory.

Two of the men had gone to help Will who was still crumpled on the floor. They each took an arm and hauled him to his feet. Together we started our slow progress towards the main street. Will's head was drooped and his bloodied hands limp as the men gripped his wrists. I could see him trying to walk, his foot taking the odd tentative step only for it to lose its purchase; his leg buckling as his foot turned awkwardly. I could hear the crowd whispering to one another, the gossip already beginning to spread.

We were heading towards the Glass Factory. The large brick structure loomed ahead, obscuring the stars. As we neared the building I could see a man illuminated by an oil lamp outside the front door. He was waiting patiently for us.

As we drew closer I began to make out Walter's large form and eventually his face by the dimly flickering flame of a hand held oil lamp. I hung back, letting everyone else enter the building. I knew Walter would want answers. He ushered me through and closed the door, locking it behind him.

"What in God's name happened!?" he shouted as he turned to face me.

I knew him well enough to know he was more upset than angry. I saw his throat tense as he swallowed, his eyes blinking wildly as he tried to reign in his sadness.

"I don't know. They were hunting her like animals," I replied, "I got a good look but didn't recognize any of them." I had to lie; I could not allow my past to follow me. Even as I spoke the words I felt a deep feeling of unease settling over me. My mind was thrown back to Devils Acre, to John stood over me, leering at me; my sister dead, lying unbreathing in her own waste; my mother hanging from the beam, her cold feet blue and swollen. I could not go back there. "They have to have been from a different part of town. She had gone to look for a place for us to stay over the winter and hadn't come back." I looked over to where they had laid Mary on the floor, Maude still fussing over her. "Until now. How is she?" I asked, raising my voice to Maude.

Lifting her head she met my eye. She did not need to utter a word; the sadness etched into the lines of her face was enough. Shaking her head she bent over to attend to her patient once more. I could hear Mary crying as her newly appointed nurse tried to calm her. I could not yet face seeing her and I felt a growing concern for Will. Still undecided, my attention was caught by a sudden commotion coming from the office. I made my way towards the noise knowing I would find Will at the centre. I did not get far before I saw him running, bloody and bruised, fighting past the men who were trying to help him.

As soon as he saw me he stopped his struggles. Running up to him I threw my arms around his neck. He winced but returned the gesture and kissed me, only briefly, on the lips.

"You're alright?" he asked anxiously, now holding me at arm's length, looking me up and down.

I nodded, studying him closely. He was hunched slightly to the right and winced in pain with every breath. They had broken some ribs. His face was a mess, the cut lip, black eye and broken nose was the least of his problems in his present state. I could see scuff marks on his arms and knuckles where he had fought back and he had broken two fingers; they had been tied to the fingers next to them as a form of support. Despite all of this his only thoughts were for Mary and me.

"What about Mary?" he asked, frantically looking around as if expecting to see her somewhere in the crowd.

My stoical smile faltered as my thoughts returned to our friend.

"What did they do to her?" he pressed when I did not reply.

"I'm sorry." Tears welled and started falling from my eyes, streaking my blood-stained face. "They raped her." My breath caught in my throat as I tried to continue. "She's there." I pointed down the factory to where I could see Maude tending her.

He took my hand as we walked towards her. Suddenly the world changed; I did not feel myself stop, or register the action in my mind. All I could hear was my breathing, all I could see was my mother and sister. I could feel all the loss and devastation all over again. I shook my head as I started backing away, my eyes never leaving the body on the floor and the nightmares conjured by my mind.

My breath came in violent gasps. Looking at Will I could see his lips moving but could not hear the words. My breaths came faster and faster as the panic began to overtake all other senses. I turned and ran, stumbling and tripping in my panic. I had to get away. I saw a door, an escape. I crashed through it, throwing it shut behind me. Slowly I realised I was in the office; I watched as a pile of papers gently drifted to the floor and littered the small office with the door's vehement slam. Scrambling behind the desk I crawled into the foot-well where I curled myself into a ball. I tried to shut out everything, all thoughts and memories, as my mother and sister swam before me once more.

In the silence I gradually began to relax, the vice-like grip around my chest easing with each breath. I felt better for the silence. My mind had a chance to consider what was happening. I lifted my hands and watched them shaking. The light was flickering between my fingers, my hands becoming indistinct with the involuntary movements.

I heard footsteps outside, coming towards the door. I knew it was Will, nobody else would have come. As the door opened I could not decide what to do. I was too embarrassed to climb out but knew I could not stay in my protective hole for ever. Before I could make up my mind the chair was dragged aside and Will was crouched in front of me, bending his head so he could make eye contact. He just looked at me. Studying his face I could see a mixture of emotions rolling in turmoil behind his calm exterior. Finally he broke the silence.

"What happened?" he asked, sadness dominating his tone.

"I…I…I don't know. It was like, my mother and sister, all over again. I was scared."

"Scared of what?" Confusion stirred within the sadness of his eyes like clouds amid a dark storm.

"What I would see."

"She needs us, now more than ever. We can't leave her." He closed his eyes as he took a breath. As he opened them I saw the mist of uncertainty clear and a steady resolve settle over him. "You have to keep it together; she's not as strong as you and me. We need to look after her. Come on, one step at a time. Just don't let go." I felt his words sink in as he looked past the terrified young woman huddled under a desk and spoke to me. He held out a steadfast hand.

I placed my hand in his and felt his warm fingers wrap around mine as he helped me to my feet. He led me through the factory, curious eyes edgily following us. I walked through the crowd, concentrating on nothing but the feel of Will's hand in mine. I felt the calluses at the base of each finger and the rough skin of his knuckles. Concentrating on these insignificant details I walked on; I could not allow myself to fall apart again.

The mass of people parted as we stepped inextricably closer. Walking into the deep void, a chill ran through my body; it was as if the sea were parting, daring me to walk between my opposing currents. I had to confront these torments. I could not lose myself; I could not lose this family as I had lost my last.

Will took the last step, kneeling down in front of Mary. He reached forward to try and straighten her torn clothing but she pulled herself back, her whole body curling inwards. Half her face was covered in dirt where her head had been pushed into the mud. She bore scratches down her neck, her chest and over her shoulder, her face swollen and bruised. I stepped to his side and crouched next to him, studying our battered friend. I found solace in the knowledge that I could be this close to my fear and not feel the burning pain of my past.

He reached out to take her hand but she withdrew, pulling her hand deeper into the folds of the blankets. She was staring at the floor, her unblinking eyes showing nothing. Will and I looked at one another. In that one look I understood. We could not return to the docks; the pain of tonight would be too great for Mary to bear. We would have to find a new home, make a new start, for us to stand any chance of saving her.

At another sideways glance and head tilt from Will I shuffled over and sat next to Mary. I did not attempt to touch her but positioned myself so that my side was pressed to hers. After a few moments I felt her weight gently rest against me. She laid her head on my shoulder and there is where we stayed. Will pushed himself to his feet and limped away. I did not move or look at her, did not dare stretch out a hand for fear of making her retreat deeper into herself.

Will soon returned, overshadowed by Walter's large frame with Alfred trailing behind them.

"You can stay here until you sort something out," Walter said as they drew closer. "We've cleared an area of the back office for you to sleep. It can't be for long though, the administrator will be back by the end of the week and he can't know that you've been here."

Nodding my acceptance to his offer I softly nudged Mary and rolled onto my hands and knees. I slowly got to my feet. I was beginning to feel the bruising and sore joints. Will and I reached out to Mary, but she pushed us away, holding up a shaking hand and eyeing us warily. She struggled to her feet, her trembling limbs barely supporting her slight frame. Steadying herself for a moment on the bench, her hand still outstretched in warning, she slowly took her first painful step.

Slowly, each of us limping and pained, we made our way to the office where they had cleared an area of the floor from the fallen papers. Mary automatically curled into a ball on the floor. I glanced at Will who gave me a wry smile before bending down, his hand hovering over her shoulder, still not daring to touch her. He withdrew his arm and stepped back, unsure what to say. He stepped out of the office, holding the door open for me to follow.

I waited until the door to the office was firmly closed before I turned to Will. "What are we going to do?" I asked desperately.

Will gave me deep searching look before taking my hand and walking towards the assembled crowd. As we walked amongst the dormant workings of the factory he wrapped his arm around my shoulders and pressed a soft kiss to my temple. "We sit tight for a while. We need to find somewhere more permanent to stay, somewhere Mary will be safe." He looked up at the crowd stood whispering in low tones. "Anyone know anywhere we could stay?" he asked the room at large.

Nobody answered.

Eventually Walter stepped forward. "There's nothing we can do tonight regardless. Just get some rest and we'll sort something out come morning." He gestured for us to go back to the office.

Alfred opened his mouth to protest, his eyes darting toward Will. Before he could speak Walter cast him a warning eye. As Alfred turned away I saw him mouth something at Walter, his arms raised in dismay. Whatever they were discussing it was obvious they did not want us involved in the conversation.

Reluctantly Will nodded his assent and led me back to the office. It was clear he wanted to move on, get Mary away from here as soon as possible, but Walter was right, there was nothing to be done until morning. Will gently pulled the door to behind us as we shuffled deeper into the room. I could not hear a sound coming from the curled outline on the floor. "Mary, Mary," I whispered, "are you okay? Can I get you anything?" Still she did not stir. I moved to place my hand on her shoulder but Will stopped me, his hand taking mine and pulling it away.

He stepped over Mary and, releasing me, sat on the floor, his back resting against the wall. He lifted his arms and gestured for me to join him. I scooted past Mary and made my way gingerly over to him. Nestling into his body I pressed my cheek to his chest. He wrapped his arms around me as he pressed his lips to my head.

"Try and sleep Clara," he whispered.

I closed my eyes and wished for sleep to take me, but sleep, it seemed, was to be an elusive beast that night. Will's breathing not once lapsed into the relaxed rhythmic breaths that only came from the depths of sleep. Mary was too still, too quiet, I doubted whether she would ever sleep soundly again. My eyes were half closed, my dilated pupils unmoving from the curved form of Mary at my feet. After many sleepless hours I finally fell into a restless doze.

Chapter 13

I awoke the next morning to find Will nowhere in sight. As I got my bearings I noticed Mary had also disappeared. I got up and, tripping on the discarded blankets, left the office in a rush. Casting my eyes around the factory I saw Alfred and Walter talking in low voices by the work bench. Walter was stood with his arms folded, resting on his large belly. His furrowed brow was personified by his confrontational stance, both feet planted firmly, his back rigid and his jaw held taught in uncontainable irritation. Alfred meanwhile was stood meek and cringing under Walter's glare. I strode purposely towards them. Slowing as I came closer, I caught a little of their conversation.

"I don't like it. She's better than that. You know what will happen!" Walter was growling.

"You don't know that. They won't push her to do anything she doesn't want to do. What other choice do they have? Will's there now sorting it out. He'll make sure they're safe. Just see what Clara thinks of it," Alfred said imploringly, stepping back as he saw Walter's eyes narrow in anger.

"Thinks about what?" I asked coming level with them. I saw Alfred give Walter a guilty look before casting his eyes to the ground.

The uneasy silence stretched on.

"It was your idea Fred. You tell her!" Walter gave me an apologetic look and backed away. Leaning against the work bench, his animosity burning through the air I breathed.

"What's the plan Alfred?" I prompted for a second time while trying to ignore my feeling of unease.

"Just hear me out before you refuse, yeah?"

"Alright, I'll hear you out," I shrugged, my eyes flicking to Walter once more.

"There's a brothel on the other side of town."

I opened my mouth to protest and he raised his hand. "You promised."

I closed my mouth, giving Alfred a steely glare.

"I went down last night and spoke to some of the girls. They'll happily take all of you in. Before you jump down my throat, they'll not ask anything like that of you. They'll take Will on as an extra doorman and you and Mary as serving girls." A deep silence followed. He stood away from me, cautious of my reaction. "So, what do you think?" he finished nervously.

"They don't expect me to be, you know, one of the girls?"

"No. I checked. I, um, used have a good working relationship with one of the girls." His face flushed crimson at his tactless explanation. "Look, just give it a chance. You can't stay on the streets; it's too dangerous, not with all those murders. There was another attack last week and now you three. There's a real nasty piece of work out there and it looks like he likes young ladies like yourself."

His words drew my mind back to the newspaper I had seen yesterday, the image of that woman cowering on the ground. How prophetic it had been, that could easily have been Mary or myself. The thought sent a shiver of fear through me that settled over my soul like a dark mist, tainting my world with its corrupt stench. I closed my eyes, pushing the image of John standing over me with a knife to the back of my mind. "Sorry, where did you say Will had gone?"

"Will's there now, just going over the formalities. You know, checking it all out, making sure he's happy with it."

"And Mary?"

"She's with Maude. Over there," he clarified, pointing to the far corner of the factory.

"Thank you." I made my way between the workers who were starting to arrive for their day's labour. For the first time I did not gaze admirably at their work as I passed. All I could see between the rising steam and volley of workers was Mary and Maude, sat on a bench by the wall.

Maude looked up as I approached and smiled. She rubbed Mary's arm and gave her a hug. Standing, she wrapped her arms around me, encompassing me in an embrace full of meaning. She gave love, comfort and strength in that one small gesture. Sitting down in her vacated seat I could think of nothing to say. I opened my mouth but words failed me. I took a deep breath; once more the words became stuck in my throat. I swallowed, my mouth dry.

"Will's gone to sort it out. You wait, by the end of the day we'll have new jobs, all be sorted," Mary stated in an odd, sing-song voice. I looked at her, my eyes wide with concern and misunderstanding. She was looking at the floor, her head tilting from one side to the other, her toes alternately tapping the air. I bent my head, trying to see the expression behind her mass of hair. Her eyes gazed around the room, moving in a strange fashion, her head tipping from side to side as she contemplated her words. Suddenly her eyes met mine and she smiled a blank, glassy smile. "Don't worry Clara, Will always sorts it out," she said, a pronounced frown marring her already beaten face. She then turned and continued her toe tapping.

"Yeah, we'll have a nice warm bed and a good income. It'll be a new start for us."

She nodded as we lapsed back into silence. As we sat, I began to hear her humming an odd, disjointed nursery rhyme. I watched as the toe tapping stopped. Slowly her feet started to move. She swung her feet off the edge of the bench, her toes scuffing the floor, making deeper scores in the dirt with each pendulum like swing. It was in time with the slowly hummed tune; the reminiscent ghost of a childhood lost.

My attention was diverted only when the front door opened, causing a cold draft to surge through the building. The smoke and steam billowed up in great clouds that rose to the rafters. As a shiver ran over my body the door slammed shut. I looked up to find Will, still bruised and battered, striding towards us. I stood as he approached; reaching out my hand I guided him back to our bench.

"The brothel is willing to hire us. I'm going to be an extra doorman. There have been a lot of attacks recently…"

"So I've heard," I butted in, shooting Will a harsh glare. I did not want the attacks mentioned in front of Mary.

With a raised eyebrow Will continued, "…and they want more security to protect the girls. All you two need to do is serve the drinks. What do you think? Do you want to start today? We could go there now if you want, can start settling in? What do you think?"

I gave a dry, hollow laugh that touched neither my heart nor my eyes.

"What do you think?" he asked indignantly, affronted by my reaction.

"It sounds like a great idea but it's up to Mary really. Do you feel ready to go? I'm sure we could stay a little longer." I looked at Mary, searching her face for a sign of her true feelings. She looked back at me, hiding any emotions she may have had behind a blank protective shell.

"Umm, they want us there today," Will muttered. He looked to the floor as he caught sight of my glare.

"I'm happy to go," Mary said as she gingerly pushed herself up to standing.

She started walking as best she could towards the door.

"Well, that solves that," Will wittered without humour. As he stood and pulled me reluctantly to my feet Walter stepped in front of us.

"Are you sure about this?" he asked in a low voice, "I'm here if you need me."

"Thank you Walter," I said. Releasing Will's hand I reached out and shook Walter's. He leant forwards and gave me a kiss on my cheek.

He then turned to Will, shook his hand and reiterated his final words to him. "You don't have to do this, we can find something else."

Will cut him off with a raised hand. "There is nothing else."

"Anything you need you know where I am," Walter continued regardless.

Will took my hand as we left, meeting Mary at the door where she was waiting for us, her arms crossed over her chest, her whole body turned away from the crowd. Turning at the door I waved goodbye to the men, who, for the last three years had been a part of our extended family. My eyes fell to the floor and I turned my back on the factory. I stepped into the rain that had started to fall sometime in the night. I leant into Will, bracing myself against the wailing wind as it rushed through the narrow alleys of the factories and through the broad bustling streets. Mary kept her distance as we walked, always keeping herself just out of reach. Together we made our way to the brothel.

We walked for most of the day. The rain slowly turned from light drops that caught in the glare of the low sun to an unrelenting, sunless downpour that cut through our skin like ice. Slowed by Mary's painful pace we arrived by late afternoon. We stopped, sopping wet and chilled to the marrow, at a nondescript door set back from the street. Its blue paint was flaking from years of neglect and a white stone pillar stood at each side of the entrance, covered in soot and small growths of moss and fungi. We huddled on the single step that led up to the front door, freed from the heavy rain by the small porch roof overhead. Will reached up, his fist hovering before the wooden door. He looked at us.

"You sure about this?"

I nodded my head, causing water to trickle down my face and drip off the tip of my nose. I would agree to anything as long as I could escape this infernal weather. He gave me one last doubtful look before knocking three times. I listened intently. Over the din of falling water I could make out the distinct noise of high heeled boots clipping over creaking floor boards. As they came nearer I started fidgeting, attempting in vain to tidy my hair. I was in the process of wiping the wet smears of dirt and leftover blood from my face and straightening my clothes when the door opened.

The owner of the brothel answered the door. The bawd was a striking woman. Her dark hair was piled high on her head and held in place with elaborate pins. I could see jewels glinting in her hair, reflecting off the soft glow of light surrounding her from a blazing fire behind. She smiled at us through a row of broken yellow teeth, her striking red lipstick seeping into the small crevices of skin surrounding her thin lips.

I noticed her dress, it was old, but well made, boned at the hips, waist and breasts to give her more of a shape. It looked tight, as if it were a size too small, her breasts barely kept at bay by the deep red silk and ruched lace. I noted the dark stains that covered the dress and a few areas around the side that showed the fabric was fraying. The skirt was gathered at one side, held high by a hidden piece of cotton, that revealed her black lace stocking held in place with a piece of red ribbon. Her high heeled boots gleamed in the light from the fire, throwing the tiny detailing and lacework into sharp relief.

Her eyes roved over us as she focused on distinct aspects of our appearance. After much scrutiny she addressed us. "So, you're the new girls then. What you waiting for? Get inside; we need to get you cleaned up." Her broad cockney accent dripped with contempt as she appraised us. With no further comment she turned on her heel and made her way back down the corridor.

I glanced at Will, feeling immediately doubtful of our decision. My concern was mirrored in his eyes but we had nowhere else to go. I nudged Mary ahead as I brought up the rear, shutting the door on the dismal weather.

The corridor was papered in richly designed paper. At the far end I could now see the great fire burning, the heat radiating from it warming me through. I felt my skin blaze as a wave of heat hit my face; I closed my eyes and allowed my body to absorb the warmth.

As we passed an open door I peered inside. Across the back wall of a large room stood a bar where a woman was serving drinks. Most of the occupants were dozing in chairs or trying to make conversation with disinterested women. I saw a woman perk up and smile at one; I questioned the reason only to see a pile of coins being deposited in her palm.

I scooted to catch up with my companions. Everywhere I looked, every room and nook was a bustle of activity and music from many sources filled the house. We followed the bawd around the corner and were faced with a grand sweeping staircase. Without hesitation she carried on up the stairs.

The downstairs decor had been continued and lining the walls were oil lamps burning in ornate brackets illuminating paintings of scantily-clad women. Most of the doors were closed but I could hear the activities continuing behind. We passed a door that stood ajar. A man was lying on the bed, a greedy expression on his face. At the foot of the bed a woman was dancing seductively, his eyes hungrily following her every move. She glanced up, distracted by my obvious curiosity. I moved quickly down the corridor, not wanting her to think I had been watching. We continued on to the end of the hallway and up another staircase. More closed doors, singing, laughing and the sounds of the women's trade. Eventually she stopped and turned to us, waiting for us to catch up.

"We can't have you looking like that. You clean yourselves up while I find you something to put on. You can start work proper tomorrow. Can't wait for you girls to settle in, I've lost four this month already, you got to look after yourselves round here," she said, eyeing Mary priggishly.

She pushed open a door to reveal our new accommodation. I stepped inside, full of trepidation; only to be pleasantly surprised. In the corner was a large rudimentary bed with two much smaller cots made up on the floor. Set into the far wall was a small fire crackling happily; its bright flickering flames licking around the glowing wood. In the middle of the room sat a large tub, full of steaming water. Placed on the rim were a bar of soap, wash cloths and clean towels.

As we walked into the room the woman indicated to the bath. "I had the bath drawn up for you; the water's not been in long. You clean yourselves up and I'll send one of the girls up to you with a fresh set of clothes," she said with a disgusted scowl at our attire before leaving the room, shutting the door firmly behind her.

Will politely ducked his head and stepped outside, leaving Mary and I to wash in private. Wrapped in towels we allowed Will to wash as we averted our eyes. We sat and talked about anything but what had happened. Gradually our forced conversation stuttered like a dying fire and silence fell between us. Mary was staring into the flames, muttering to herself. I looked to Will. I could see the concern in his wide eyes as he regarded her, the fire light dancing off her unmoving irises. The trance was broken when a plain looking girl walked in, barely able to see over the top of her overladen arms.

"Here, ma'am told me to give you these to try on. Got some shirts for night and chores and some dresses for the punters. See what you think of them." She deposited her load onto our bed and backed out again, curtseying at the door.

Will and I dived into the pile, grabbing a long work shirt and knickerbockers each and dragging them on before handing a set to Mary. Delving deeper Will found a white shirt, black waist coat and black trousers. He also had a pair of black leather shoes and white socks. He held them up to his body and was satisfied by this simple gesture that they would fit.

Mary sat and started picking through the pile of clothes. I saw her shift slightly as she spotted a light blue dress. "You like this one?" I asked, pulling it out and holding it up. "It would suit you, and look here's a dark blue one for me. Fancy that, us girls all made up and wearing real dresses." I tried to laugh but stopped quickly as Mary's lips refused to lift.

In the pile I found stockings, jewellery, heeled boots and more. I took my chosen items to the corner and folded them neatly. The only item from the streets I kept was the bag Will had given me, the rest I placed by the door to be given to someone who needed them more than I did now.

Once we had tried on our clothes, marvelled at the soft fabrics and the way they showed off our bodies we dragged ourselves into our long night shirts and climbed into the bed. Will lay in the middle and I curled up with his arm around me, my head resting on his shoulder, my back to the room. Mary huddled in the corner of the bed facing the shedding wallpaper and damp covered wall, her back resolutely turned towards Will.

Despite all that had happened and the emotions that rolled in turmoil beneath my fragile skin, I was exhausted. As I lay in Wills arms I felt my limbs sink into the bed, my muscles relaxed and heavy. I fell into a sound sleep where, for once, I was not haunted by the demons of my past.

Chapter 14

My eyes opened to an unknown room; my immediate emotion one of confusion as I tried to place the large metal tub and the rocking chair in the corner with some unrecognisable clothes were draped over it. As I dragged my hair away from my face my eyes came to rest on the small, tightly curled form of Mary, sleeping on one of the small cots made up on the floor.

Will stirred beside me. I felt him twist in bed before violently sitting up. As his eyes found Mary he stilled.

"You thought she had gone?" I whispered, looking up at him.

"I don't know what I thought," he muttered darkly as he rubbed his eyes with the backs of his hands. "I didn't even feel her move," he continued, looking to where she had been curled the night before.

A gentle tap at the door pulled Will from his troubled thoughts. A young woman poked her head around the door, her long mahogany locks falling over her shoulder. "Morning," she said with an air of sarcastic cordiality. "I'm Freda. You got the stuff from Mary-Jane then," she said, eyeing the clothes on the chair. "Ma'am wants you up and ready for breakfast as soon as, well now."

"We'll be right with you," Will said.

Freda's gaze reluctantly slid to Will and appraised him, a slight frown marring her otherwise flawless skin. With pursed lips she looked from Will to Mary's silent form on the small bed of rags. "Ma'am said she doesn't have to come down, one of the girls can bring her up something, you two got some work to do."

With an exaggerated breath she flashed Will and I an unconvincing smile and shut the door with a snap.

"What was all that about?" I asked as we clambered out if bed.

"I have no idea," Will answered. "Let's get down to breakfast."

"Mary," I walked over and laid my hand on her shoulder, "Mary, we're going down to breakfast, we'll bring something back for you, or," I corrected myself, "one of the girls will. Rest well." I kissed the soft pads of my fingers and pressed them to the side of her head.

We made our way downstairs guided by raised voices coming from what proved to be the kitchen. We walked through the door to mixed reactions. Some stopped and gawped freely, looking us up and down, others ignored us completely while others whispered behind hands and threw us anxious glances.

"Here, you can sit by me," the girl from last night said, giving us a warm smile, "I'm Mary-Jane."

As we slid into a couple of the empty chairs that were bunched haphazardly around the rough wooden table I noted Will was next to Freda. I watched from the corner of my eye as she turned her body subtly away from him.

Women, men and young girls surrounded the table. They were sat on one another's laps and helping themselves to each other's food. As I ate I listened to snippets of conversation around the table.

"I know, they said he hacked out parts of her body. Different bits from the girls. Ain't that right Georgey Boy," a woman said with a lavish smile and wink down the table as she sat sprawled over the young man's lap.

"Everyone's looking for him, won't be long until he's found," he answered levelly. He caught my eye as he finished his sentence, holding my gaze in his dark irises.

"Yeah but that's the fourth he's killed, that we know about. Mark my words, it'll be more," the woman said, dragging his thoughts back to her.

Disturbed by the conversation I turned my attention to the other end of the table and away from Georgey Boy's assessing gaze.

"You think the bawd will let us see the show? The Elephant Man, I've heard he gives people nightmares!" Freda was saying, leaning forward, her eyes wide with excited ecstasy.

"I've heard he screams at the crowd. He's mad, a real mad man!" said another girl with bright golden locks. Grabbing Freda's arm she gave her an excited shake, a mischievous grin that showed her innocent captivation spreading across her face.

"I'll ask Harry if he'll take us," Freda answered.

This conversation was not much better. My feelings were mixed regarding the open ridicule of someone less fortunate. Luckily my interest was diverted by a sudden roar of laughter from the corner.

"And I said, if that's all you've got I'll only charge you half!"

An even louder roar of laughter followed the punch line of this story.

As breakfast wound down from rapturous laughter and tactless talk to quiet contemplation and stifled yawns, people began to leave the table. When the room was almost void of men and women Mary-Jane approached, us her hazel eyes sparkling. On closer inspection she was not plain at all. "Clara, I've been told to show you around."

"And you're with me young William," a booming voice called as a mountain of a man approached us, "I'm Harry."

"Nice to meet you Harry." Will offered him his hand. "Please, call me Will. So, what's first?"

Harry smiled at Will's enthusiasm, showing two broken front teeth. They made their way to the door. Will stopped, momentarily placing his hand on my shoulder and giving it a reassuring squeeze before following Harry out.

I followed Mary-Jane, her mousy brown hair bouncing as she hopped up the stairs to the bar that was above the basement kitchen. It was warm and charming with dark-stained pine flooring, ornate silver oil lamps and heavy-lined curtains of the deepest red that pooled on the floor. The room was full of mismatched chairs and tables, but each held the same feeling of simple comfort. Mary-Jane led me to the bar, which, like the floor, was made of highly-polished pine with delicate detailing around the edge. Despite the clean, sumptuous surrounding I could feel indentations and scratches in the wood as I ran my hand over the bar. On the corners the wood had been chipped and scraped, the light, untreated pine showing through like a dusty yellow ore of gold in an unremarkable wall of rock.

As the men began to arrive Mary-Jane started taking me through the drinks and pricing. I could see she was an old hand at the business, the way she flowed around the room, barely looking at where her hands were going to quickly grab glasses and drinks. She was well trained, her movements soft and seductive as she reached for the high glasses and leant against the bar when pouring the drinks. It seemed to come naturally to her.

Her talents were personified by my disordered actions. My hands fumbled the glasses clumsily and I struggled with the measures of drink. She was patient as she taught me the basics of the work, talking in a low voice and pointing discreetly at the correct bottle. As we worked the bar the women worked the floor. It was obvious a lot of them had regulars and even I could spot the neophyte standing awkwardly at the door. One of the women took pity on him and walked over, confident and slow, her dress low, her eyes fixed on him. She took him by the hand and led him to a table where she sat whispering in his ear.

As the last man left Mary-Jane sent me to the kitchen to heat some water and bring it up with soap and cloths for cleaning. I made my way down the stairs but halted at the door, hearing raised voices within.

"Not for me. It's up to you, dunno if it's worth it, they looked pretty set to me." A long silence followed.

"Anyone's worth a go, anyway, what she got that I ain't?"

"I think it's what she don't have that you do that would be more to the point."

"Oi! You watch your mouth, you're no better, and she's no prettier neither."

I faked a stumble and rattled the door before stepping inside. I had a creeping suspicion Will and I were the focus of their conversation and I would have preferred not to find myself in a confrontation the first night on the job.

The girls stopped talking as I stepped through the door. "Evening, Freda, isn't it?" I asked, keeping my voice light and my face clear of my true thoughts. Freda didn't answer and I continued on as if I had not noticed her obvious hostility. "I'm sorry; I don't know your name?" I asked looking at the young woman perched on a stall, scrubbing clothes in a large metal tub.

"Ida," the young woman clarified. She had intelligent green eyes and a knowing smile to match. I got the feeling she knew I had been listening. "Anything else you need Freda?" she asked.

"No, just make sure you get the stains out this time," she snapped before turning to leave the room. She sauntered towards the door, where I was still standing in the entrance. It was clear she had no intension of asking me politely to move. I turned so my back was against the frame and she breezed past.

"Have a lovely evening," I called to her retreating back, unable to keep the sarcasm from my voice.

"Ignore her," Ida said as I turned back into the room. "She's just jealous," she scoffed as she brushed her auburn hair from her face.

"Jealous of what?"

"You and Will," she stated as if it were obvious, her hair again falling across her face as she continued to scrub the dresses. With a soapy, wet hand she pushed her hair behind her ear once more and continued to smile up at me. Thankfully my perplexed expression prompted her to continue. "We're normally not allowed to, you know, get to know the men that work here, but since you two were already…" Ida paused, looking at my increasingly bewildered expression, "ma'am excused it. Will must have been mighty persistent when he came to talk to her the other day."

"Okay, so why is there a problem?" I asked while wondering what sort of relationship everyone thought we had and what exactly Will had discussed while Mary and I were back at the glass factory.

"Well, you know what it's like, rules are rules, but as long as it doesn't get in the way of us working the bawd doesn't really mind. With Will she obviously saw a problem already brewing, Freda was all over him when he came here first, and umm, she reminded us all of the rules here. Freda's not too happy about it is all."

I could think of no response to her explanation. Thankfully she could see me floundering. "Did you come down here for something, or were you looking for a showdown with the tenacious Miss Freda?"

"Bowl of water and some soap for cleaning down," I answered laughing.

By the time I made my way to bed late that evening my head was pounding with the new information I had taken in. Will caught up with me on the stairs. "Clara, hay, Clara," he called as he bounded up the staircase two at a time. "Busy day?" he asked as he fell into step beside me.

I slid my arm into his and leaned against his shoulder. "I'm beat, didn't stop all day, only got to eat when food was brought up for the men."

"I know the feeling. Harry had me carting food and beer all day." Will rubbed his neck and arched back as he tried to release the tension in his shoulders. "You wouldn't believe how big the basement is beside the kitchen, goes right back to the far end of the house, there's another entrance back there too," he said pointing towards the back of the house as he pushed our bedroom door open.

He held the door open for me before following me in. I drifted lazily to the bed and rolled onto the soft lumpy mattress, not even bothering to take off my boots. Will kicked off his shoes and flopped down beside me.

"Where's Mary?" Will asked, propping himself up on his elbows and looking around the room as if expecting to see her lurking in one of the corners. "Have you seen her today?"

"No, I couldn't leave the bar, she never came down."

Will was already climbing out of bed and pushing his feet back into his discarded shoes, a look of concern chiselled into his tensed jaw and furrowed brow. "I'm going to look for her. Where would she have gone?" he muttered more to himself than to me.

"Hold your horses, I'm coming," I yawned.

I crawled out of bed and took Will's outstretched hand, his fingers curled and uncurled in restless anxiety as we jogged to the door. As Will's hand reached for the handle the door opened. Mary was stood in the hall looking lost and bemused. I felt Will relax as his eyes swept over her. Her face was swollen and the bruising now held court over the rest of her face but the scratches had scabbed over and there were no new injuries to be seen.

"Where have you been?" Will asked, stepping back to allow her in.

"Here and there," she said, her head tilting from side to side as she looked at us. "Were you worried?" she asked eventually.

"Of course we were bloody worried. For crying out loud Mary!" Will ran his hand through his hair, his head shaking as he turned away from us. "You can't just go like that. We need to know where you are."

"Why?"

"To make sure you're safe. Look, you're not well, you need your rest. The bawd wanted you to stay in here until you're better."

"She knew where I was."

"What do you mean?" I asked. "Who knew where you were?"

"The bawd. She knows where I was and it's got nothing to do with you."

"Where have you been Mary?" Will asked, my concern mirrored in his tone.

"Like I said, it's nothing to do with you. Ma'am trusts me, she needs me. She's even given me my own room."

At first I was not sure what she meant until she turned to leave.

"Mary, wait," I called.

She turned back and looked at me with blank eyes. My stomach rolled with unease.

"No. We want you to stay here, with us," Will said, his arm reaching out to her, his eyes wide with concern.

She stepped away from him. "No!" she shouted as fear flashed across her face.

"I would never hurt you," Will said as his hand fell to his side. "Mary, please stay."

Uttering not a word she turned away from us, collected what remained of her clothing and left the room.

"She, she can't do that!" Will half shouted, pointing at the closed door, his face furrowed in pain. His eyes looked wild and lost as he felt our friend slipping away. "She can't, I mean, why would she?"

"Let her go Will," I sighed. "We can't stop her. After what she's been through, just give her time."

I could see the anguish in his body, he looked defeated; his whole body slumped and withered as he pushed his hands deep into his pockets. "We've never been apart, not since the workhouse," he murmured.

"Come now Will, there is nothing to be done. She has made her choice; all we can do now is respect it. Come to bed. I wouldn't be surprised to wake up tomorrow and see her sleeping beside us."

I pulled a hand out of his pocket and led him back to bed. As he sat on the edge I bent down and untied his shoes, I pulled them off along with his socks and started unbuttoning his shirt. Eventually he helped, pulling the shirt off his shoulders and standing to undo his trousers.

"Bed, now," I said as if I were talking to a small child.

With a wry smile he climbed into bed and watched as I stripped to my underdress and crawled in next to him.

"Try and sleep Will. Mary will come through, I promise," I said as I lay my head on his chest.

"Whatever it takes," Will whispered back as he kissed the top of my head.

I awoke the next morning to find myself encased in Will's arms. I opened my eyes to see Will staring over my head, into the room. I turned my head and followed his gaze. He was looking at the two makeshift cots on the floor. They were empty. "She didn't come back."

"No," Will answered, his eyes not moving from the cold, unkempt beds.

"I thought she would come back."

"So did I," he uttered.

As I got my limbs untangled from the plentiful bedding Will clambered over me. He was dressed and waiting by the door before I had dragged my work shirt over my head.

"Please stop worrying Will, Mary will be at breakfast," I said, feeling uncomfortable as the tension radiating from him intensified the further we walked through the house.

"Don't you think it's a little odd? I've been thinking about what Mary said, about the bawd knowing where she was."

"Yes," I answered levelly, not wanting to show Will how concerned I was. I had spent half the night lying awake, running Mary's words through my head. Our conversation halted as we walked down the stairs towards the basement.

We stepped into the kitchen to find it full. Mary was at the far end of the table sat between Freda, whose hair was tied into small curled bunches with rags, and the bawd. She didn't look up as we entered and crammed ourselves in at the end of the bench. As we helped ourselves to food Will called, "morning Mary," without looking up.

"Morning," she said, appraising us coolly.

"Did you sleep well last night?"

Rather than answer she looked at Freda who turned her head away from us and muttered something to her. Will cleared his throat and looked at her expectantly, his face remaining resolutely passive as his hand clenched into a tight fist, his knuckles standing out, pearly white, through his skin.

"Yes, Freda kept me company."

"Anyway," Freda butted in, "we have important work to do, don't we Mary."

As Freda stood Mary followed, still limping slightly, out of the room. Will started to rise, his intentions clear.

"Will, you're with Harry, Clara, you're with Mary-Jane," the bawd cut across the room.

Will looked at me and I gave the smallest shake of my head, the warning clear in my eyes. Whatever was going on with Mary, we were not going to find out unless we played along. One wrong word and we could be on the streets again and then we would have no way of protecting Mary. "Yes ma'am," I answered, my eyes not leaving Will's.

"Of course Ma'am," Will eventually said, his eyes leaving mine to lock with the mistress of the house.

"You'll find Harry out back and Mary-Jane in the bar," she dismissed.

Will picked up the piece of bread he had been eating and stalked from the room without so much as a backwards glance.

"Thank you ma'am," I said with a bob of my head before cutting off a piece of bread for myself and scurrying from the room.

Chapter 15

Over the weeks that followed Mary continued to distance herself from us as she got closer to Freda. We worked at the bar together most nights but she would barely talk and her moods would come and go with the passing of clients. Sometimes she would be lucid and talkative, joking with the girls as they worked the floor. Other days she would stare blankly at the wall and flinch at the slightest touch. Then came the days when she would disappear completely, usually going off with Freda or one of the other girls, no explanation given and nothing to show for the absent nights.

Despite our concerns Will and I found ourselves being drawn more towards Mary-Jane and Ida. Ida had a quick wit and an eye for detail, always able to pick out the ones who could pay. Not a prostitute herself, like us she was a barmaid and cleaner, but she was the one the girls called on to pick out a good punter for the night.

Although I was still new to the trade I was beginning to get to know the job. I still struggled to remember what drinks people had ordered and who I was serving, but I was slowly improving under Mary-Jane's patient tuition. As the evenings wore on the men got more intoxicated and just understanding what they were ordering was hard work. Thankfully Ida taught me a good trick that left the practice of understanding them redundant. She went by the smell of their breath as to whether they were after a pint of beer or something a bit stronger.

The women were well practiced at getting the men to part with their money. They would offer just enough to make them eager and then ask for more money for them to continue.

As the church bells tolled for midnight it began to settle down and I started cleaning down the bar. I was polishing glasses when Will came in, pulling up a stool. "Penny for your thoughts?" I asked. He looked exhausted. "And a drink," I added pouring a large measure of whiskey.

"Well, that was an interesting night" he said, taking what looked to be a well-earned stretch; his tired eyes barely noticing me.

I glared at him, my hands on my hips, my newly fashioned eyebrows raised in amused annoyance. After a few moments he did a double take. "Your dress, sorry." I could see him trying to find the appropriate response through his fog of exhaustion. "You look amazing! Look at you, all grown up and looking like a lady!" he said appraisingly as he scrutinised the new dress Mary-Jane had forced me into that evening.

"Alright, enough Will. Thank you for noticing my dress. I am so grateful you are such an observant, complimentary gentleman," I laughed with a well-humoured roll of my eyes.

"All joking aside, you really do look amazing you know," he smiled as he leant forwards on his elbows and stretched before rocking back onto the chair with a sigh.

Will sat and nursed his drink as I finished cleaning down the bar. Every time I looked up he was watching me, his eyes brooding and intense. As I finally finished my evening chores I walked around the bar and slipped my arm into his, my hand nestled happily in the crook of his elbow. I leant my head against his arm as we dragged ourselves upstairs to bed.

As the fire burnt low and the lamps were extinguished silence descended upon the house. Slowly, as the hours slid by, the wind picked up and the rain began to fall, lashing against the window as the wind howled on.

"What's wrong?" Will asked, speaking into the darkness, his voice hushed under the turbulent storm rolling through the night.

I had lain awake for hours, unaware that Will was sharing my sleepless night.

"Can't sleep, roll over and get some rest." I whispered, stifling a yawn.

"I would but that's the third time you've elbowed me in the back." I could feel the emotion hidden behind his teasing tone. He moved towards me, pulling me against him, his arms winding around me. I bowed tighter into my ball until I was curled like a harvest mouse around his arm, using his body and the blankets as my nest. We lay, warm and comfortable, as the storm thrashed their elements against our window. I could hear the hinges protesting as the wood creaked, the curtains billowing out as a cold, heavy gust heaved its way through the cracks.

"Try and sleep," he whispered simply as he leant his weight against me.

I felt him breathe. The hair on the back of my neck rising as the warmed air ignited my skin. A smile worked its way across my face, my eyes closing in the comfort of his arms. I nestled into him and felt his arms tighten around me. My legs leisurely stretched down from where they had been curled tightly to my chest. My toes found his feet. I immediately flinched away, drawing my legs away from the icy skin. I heard him laugh as his feet searched out mine, looking for a warm friend. With a resigned sigh I ran my feet down his legs, the hair tickling the bottoms of my feet, until I found his once more.

We lay for an age, his lips, his nose, pressed to the back of my neck. His arms were wrapped around me, one hand clasping mine where it was held to my chest, the other wound around my stomach and tucked under my waist; our feet touching and rubbing, my furnace fired blood warming his cold, overworked feet.

I felt him shift behind me as his nose nestled in my hair, his lips parting as he set a soft kiss upon my neck.

"Will," I whispered.

"Clara." I heard the soft laugh hidden behind my name. He pulled my hand away from my chest and shifted. I moved with him, rolling onto my back. With my head on his shoulder he kept our intertwined hands raised. He gently twisted our hands, watching the movements of the shadows, how our fingers morphed into one another under the muted light of the solitary oil lamp. I looked at Will, at the way his lips changed shape subtly with unspoken words and the hint of a hidden smile, his eyes never leaving our hands.

He loosened his grip, his fingers now tracing tiny patterns on my palms, tracing my heart and life lines, tracing the scars from so many days hard labour. Slowly he brought my hand to his lips, setting a soft kiss upon the back of my hand. I turned, my head still resting on his arm, facing him, my body resting against his. Slowly, like the first growth of a spring flower after a hard winter's frost, I felt my heart warm and a vital hope spring from the darkness where it settled over my tainted soul and began to take root.

The fire inside me seemed to burn from within my soul, seeping into my heart, causing my breath to halt and stutter before the fire consumed me once more. The heat seeped into every muscle and sinew of my body; it made my world stop and readjust, putting Will at the centre. He pulled himself onto his elbow. Hovering over me he bent and his lips touched mine. I heard my heart beat as his hand caressed my face, his touch scarring my skin with his fervour. His fingers trailed through my hair, down, over my breast, my waist, my hips, down my thigh, coming to rest at the back of my knee. He pulled my leg over his body as he rolled onto his back. I leant over him and trailed my fingers across his chest as I kissed him. He pulled my underdress over my head, depositing it on the floor with a careless flick of his hand. I leant down and pressed my lips to his once more.

As the light from the lamp diminished Will became my light. In a life filled with endless night he became my endless day, lighting my path, burning my past and making stars alight in the darkest corners of my soul.

Suddenly there was a hammering on the door. I leapt from the bed, my heart pounding, fear surging through my veins.

"Up, up, you must wake up!" It was the bawd.

"Yes ma'am," I called as I dragged my underdress over my head. Will was beside me, deftly pulling on his trousers and tucking in his shirt. We had ourselves dressed and somewhat presentable in a matter of seconds.

"Yes ma'am," Will reiterated as we opened the door.

The bawd took in our appearance, her eyes travelling down my disheveled clothing and the state of my hair. "If that is all you're after we have men willing to pay a pretty penny," she said through thin lips. "Come. I need you up, out and lending a hand. Go find Harry; he'll give you your instructions."

"What about Mary?" Will asked.

She gave us a scolding look. "She has her orders," she eventually conceded before turning away. We were dismissed.

As we ran down the stairs more of the girls joined us but Mary was nowhere in sight. We followed the throng of women and girls to the front door where Harry was holding court. "Right, you all know what you're doing. Nobody gets left behind, nobody goes in for an extra penny and nobody breathes a word. Go, I'll expect you back within," he pulled a tarnished watch out of the breast pocket of his waist coat, "three hours."

I saw a couple of the girls look to one another in dismay. Harry held up a hand, silencing them before they could utter a word. "I know it's not long but it's now twenty past two and I want you back before the streets get busy. Stay close and stay clean." He opened the door and allowed them to file out in silence, their heads bowing as they stepped into the gale that was howling outside.

Once the women had left he turned to look at us. Assessing us through narrowed eyes with a brow lifted speculatively in unasked questions he said, "I've got a job for you two."

"Right?" Will answered, obviously unsure.

"We're cutting it fine getting the shipment in in time, we're going to need some lookouts."

"What shipment?" Will asked.

"Never mind that, all I need you two to do is stand at either end of the street with these oil lamps and if there's no one around keep it black, if you see or hear anything open the side and signal to the end of the road."

Harry held up an oil lamp for each of us that had been completely encased in metal with a hatch on a small hinge on one side. An old piece of cloth had been wrapped around the handle and he was careful not to burn me as he handed it over. "Here," he said, passing me a small metal instrument. It was like a small spoon but held a hook on the end rather than a bowl. "To open the hatch," he explained. "With all the metal it can get a fair bit warm."

Looking closer I saw a small eye for the hook to fit into. I pushed the hook into it and lifted the hatch open. Inside a bright yellow flame danced amid the fiery tomb of metal causing the light to shatter into a thousand pieces and shine from the vessel like a small star.

"Off you go now," Harry prompted. "Clara, you're at that end," he pointed to the far corner of the street, "and Will, you stand down the other way, by that ally all the mongers cut through. Stay this side so you can see each other's light. Only open it if you see someone coming. Flash it once then get out the way. Anyone spots you, you don't work here, alright?"

I nodded silently at the threat in his tone. Harry did not need to raise his voice to be heard, every syllable resonated with terrifying sincerity.

"Alright, alright, we'll do it." Will held out his hand to me and went to lead me out the door. "Just make sure Mary gets back okay," he asked as he stopped by the door. Harry nodded his head but said nothing, instead looking pointedly to the door.

"Make sure those don't go out," he said as we stepped out into the blistering cold. The wind whipped past me, chilling me to my core. I took a breath as the rain hit my face, spluttering over me as it drained from the roof.

"Let's get this done and get back," Will shouted over the hounding gale.

I gave a last brief nod before starting up the cold dark street. The wind howled around me, my skirts rising up and floundering about my legs, making me trip on the wayward fabric. I hauled my shawl around my shoulders, desperate to keep hold of it, and kept the lantern close to my chest.

When I finally reached the end of the road I turned. I could see no hint of Will at the other end and was tempted to flash the light just so I could see him but the thought of possible repercussions stilled my hand. Instead I huddled into the wall, kept my head down and waited.

The rain intensified as the minutes ticked slowly by. I was soaked through to my skin, my sodden clothes dripping with bitter water. In the dead of night and all alone my mind began to play tricks on me. Every swath of rain was a moving shadow and every dark corner held a set of penetrating eyes. The howling wind was a woman's soulful cry and every roll of thunder a reminder of the fragility of life.

I was stood, tentatively placing one hand at a time against the hot metal of my lantern, when I stilled. It was the scrape of a boot? Or was it the scour of debris blown by the wind? I heard it again, followed by a gravelly breath. But, was that the wind rasping my ears? Caught in the clutch of fear I fumbled to get the hatch open. As my numbed fingers flailed in their endeavor my breath caught in my throat. The small loop was nowhere to be found. I lost my grip. The lamp fell to the floor with a clatter that stung my heart into a rapid beat upon my chest.

"No!" I screamed as I fell to my knees, the cobbles cold and hard beneath my exposed skin. I grabbed the lantern and turned it over, desperate to open the hatch. I struggled, the lever lost in the dark puddles as my fingers dug uselessly at the cooling metal.

A hand grabbed my shoulder. I screamed and fell forward, my shoulder coming into painful contact with the wall I had been leaning on all night.

"Shh, it's me," Will soothed.

"What in almighty's name's going on here?" Harry thundered, his voice suddenly filling the night air.

"I'm sorry, I dropped it," I stammered. "I was trying to signal but I lost my hold."

"Was someone here?" Harry barked, immediately on guard.

"Yes, well no. I don't know. I thought so, but now. This wind, rain, I can't see, can't hear my own thoughts, let alone someone sneaking around."

"Someone was sneaking?" Harry pressed. Stepping back he searched the bleak streets with roving eyes.

"I don't know. I thought I heard someone around the corner," I called over the lashing rain as I looked up at his stony face.

Harry immediately walked to the corner, seemingly oblivious to the rain lashing against his skin, and peered into the darkness. "Whoever it was, I don't think they stuck around." He was shielding the rain from his eyes, looking from us, to the street, to the brothel. He picked up the extinguished lamp and passed it to me. "Hold it close to your chest and put your back to the wind."

I did as he asked, not relishing the cold wind against my back. It made every breath painful as I gulped the frosty air into my protesting lungs.

Holding out his other hand for Will's lamp he pulled a match from an inside pocket and opened the lit lantern. He gently lay the match in the flame. With a small hiss it flashed into life. Staying hunched over the lantern to shield the stuttering ember he moved the match to mine and placed it against the wick. As it blazed once more he twisted the dial on the side, turning it first up so the flames licked the top of the lantern, then down to a bright orange glow at the base of the lamp.

"I'll stay here. Clara, you go with Will. Stand together, keep watch, look out for my signal."

Neither of us said anything. Will took me by the elbow and walked with me, past the brothel, to the end of the road.

"Go in there." Will pressed me into the wall where I was sheltered by a small overhang. I leant into the wall, my sodden clothes sticking to me as I watched Will. He stood, his back straight, his eyes bright and watchful, as the rain hammered down.

"Why are we here?" I asked.

"I don't know. I'm more worried about why we are here and Mary's not," he said, glancing at me. "I don't like it."

"If you don't like it, why are we still stood here?"

"I think they're using Mary for something. She's keeping something from us and I think the bawd has something to do with it." He stopped and gave me a deep penetrating look. "We can't force it out of Mary but we can play along and do some digging ourselves."

"So that's why we're stood here, in the middle of the night, in the torrential rain? To gain their trust?"

"Yes. Being a drudge has a bright side. People soon forget you exist and then forget their mouths when you're around," he said with a sardonic smile.

We lapsed into silence, with nothing to accompany us but the pouring rain and cruel wind. We stood, watchful and waiting as the minutes ticked by. Slowly our world brightened as the sun rose, hidden behind the mass of cloud that coveted the sky. As dawn overcame night the heavy rain dissipated into a heavy drizzle. The miniscule drops clung to Will's drenched hair causing the dark strands to glow softly in the muted light coming from the now lit windows across the street. Before long I was able to make out the steeple of the church, its dark cross etched into the sky by the nail of God, its façade bringing torment and endless pain to women of our kind.

I looked up the street and was startled from my dark thoughts by Harry striding towards us in the early morning mist. "Right, time for you two to get inside, there'll be a hot bath waiting for the both of you." He held up his arm, gesturing for us to accompany him. He said nothing of the night's escapades as we walked back to the brothel.

Past exhausted we dragged our sodden, freezing feet up the stairs, past the women who chose to catch a few men on the way to work and past the girls scrubbing the bar and polishing the glasses. Thankfully the old metal tub was waiting for us full of warmed water with soap and wash cloths.

I sank into the heavenly water, my eyes closed in ecstasy as it burned life back into my toes. Will stripped off his outer layers, leaving them in the soggy pile that already held my dress and shawl and started setting out clean, dry clothes.

"Come on. I'm still freezing here," Will said, calling me back from my thoughts of how our night had started.

I turned and smiled at him and saw the answering lift of his cheeks. He sauntered over to the bath and held out a towel, his head tilted in question. I pursed my lips and shook my head, laughing as I sunk deeper into the water.

"Alright, have it your way," he laughed before pitching himself sideways into the water and rolling on top of me.

I squealed as his cold body hit mine, the water from his hair coursing down my chest.

"Ah," he sighed as I fought to get him off me.

"Will," I cried indignantly. "Will get up, I am not laughing!" I cried, though my ribs protested as a giggle escaped my lips.

Eventually I gave up the fight and shifted until he was sitting in front of me. He pulled the shirt off over his head and lay back against me, my arms round his waist, his head resting on my shoulder.

"I'm getting cold," I whispered into the silence.

"Me to," he answered, turning his head, "You really want to get up?"

"No."

"Come on," he sighed as he pulled himself forwards and stood up, reaching for the towels. I could see his muscles ripple and tense under his lean frame, the years of hard work sculpting his body, drying out his hands and giving him the wisdom and understanding that can only come from hard years on the streets. In some ways he was so young, like how he was always looking for the next adventure or a new challenge, yet at the same time he was such an old soul, his eyes careful and yet full of sincere understanding. I was pulled from my reminiscent thoughts as he wrapped the towel around himself and stepped out of the bath, only now removing his pants. He held open the other towel for me and I gladly stepped into it.

"I don't think they're expecting us to be down for work until this afternoon," Will said, brushing the hair away from my face with tender fingers.

He walked me backwards to the bed and as the backs of my knees hit the mattress we tumbled back, a mass of hands, limbs, lips and towels.

* * *

A hot draft blows through the window and I am pulled reluctantly from my memories of those nights with Will. The drums have slowed to a steady beat, almost seductively calling the Fa forwards. A lone drum beats on and a man calls through the air. It is a declaration of adoration that is mirrored in the answering hum from those assembled.

As the cloth that has been hung over the doorway billows in an unfelt breeze a shiver runs through me. I look down at the last words I have written.

The words begin to spill into one another as slowly my tears fall into the wet ink. I wipe my cheeks with the back of my hand and gently dab at the smearing words.

I must finish what I started.

Chapter 16

I awoke late morning. As I slowly raised my head from the soft pillow I looked across to see Will snoring next to me, still lost in his oblivion. He gave a grunt and shuffled his head before finally opening his eyes. He smiled as he gazed at me, lost in thought.

"It's time to get up," I said, making no effort to move.

"I know." Rolling away from me he sat on the edge of the bed and dragged on his trousers.

I slipped out of bed behind him and pulled my dress over my head. We stepped out of the room while I still lacing up the back of my dress. Yawning we made our way through the house and down to the kitchen.

"Where's Mary?" I asked as we walked through the door. She was not sat in her usual place by Freda.

"She don't wanna come down this morning. She feels sick is all," Freda shrugged.

"What do you mean sick?" Will asked.

"You know, sick. Not feeling well. She'll be fine; you ought to be worrying about yourselves rather than other people that have nothing to do with you."

"She has everything to do with me."

"You've got no time for that now, you've got work to do. Up and cleaning the lot of you," the bawd called from the door, she must have followed us in.

"Yes ma'am." The apology was muttered around the table along with a sudden frenzy of activity as chairs were scraped back, hunks of bread ripped away from loaves and water was hastily glugged. Within seconds the table was empty as we scurried to our respective duties.

Neither Will nor I managed to check on Mary that afternoon and as a heavy blanket of cloud settled over London the sky slowly turned grey and shadows crept across the street as people hurried home before the rain began to fall. The heavens turned steel and the rain came, lashing against the windows as the whole house seemed to creak under the strain of another storm. As darkness fell Mary emerged. Her eyes were red and swollen and her hands shaking as she pulled nervously at her shawl. She said nothing as she came around the bar and started tidying glasses, the thin glass chiming an unmelodious tune as her hands quaked.

"How are you feeling?" I asked, reaching past her to wipe down the bar.

Turning away she said nothing, bending down on the pretence of taking out extra candles for the tables.

"Are you feeling the cold?" I asked rubbing my hand down her back. She had covered her small frame with a thick woollen shawl that she had wrapped loosely around herself.

Again she did not answer. Shrugging away from my touch she took the candles and holders and started setting them on the tables. As the men began to arrive I could not question her further but kept an ear trained in her direction.

Mary did well, she did not manage a smile but she kept the bar stocked and the glasses clean as Ida and I served the drinks. It was just beginning to wind down when Ida gave me a nudge and pointed to the far corner. A couple of women, including the bawd, were sat in deep discussion with a group of men. They drank, but not enough to lose their inhibitions, and they did not seem fuelled by their animalistic frustrations. They were pulling documents from inside pockets and concentrating on what looked to be long manuscripts.

I watched as a man noted something down on a sheet of paper and pushed it across the table to one of the women. The woman took it in her hand, gave it a single glance and pushed it back, shaking her head. This was followed by frantic hand gestures, much more frenzied scribbling and another exchange of notes. This time the woman nodded her head, a small smile playing across her lips. They shook hands and the gentlemen left. "Wonder what all that was about?" Ida whispered as she leaned in close on the pretence of giving me more glasses to put away.

"Don't know." I eyed the men thoughtfully as they shuffled out of the brothel, pulling their hats low over their faces as the left.

Whatever they were doing it was not to be widely acknowledged. Usually all the orders and finances were done down in the kitchen or in the bawds study, not under the light of a low lit oil lamp on a dark evening.

Suddenly a scream cut through me. The glass I was holding fell from my grasp and shattered on the floor. I whipped my head around to see Mary crouched on the floor. Her hair was straining at the roots as her hands grasped her head. Pulling and wrenching, the tiny follicles snapped and sprung free from her scalp. Her eyes were screwed shut as she continued to scream.

"I didn't do nofin, I swear, I didn't do nofin," a man was saying, his hands held up in front of him as though we had him at knife point. He backed away from the bar slowly before stumbling, turning and briskly joining his friends at a table.

"Shhh Mary shhh, what's wrong," I asked. Stepping carefully over the broken glass I crouched down next to her and tried to still her flailing hands.

"Don't touch me, don't touch me, don't touch me," she shrieked, shaking her head manically from side to side.

"MARY!" Will shouted as he ran around the bar. "Mary what is it? What happened?"

"NO! Don't touch me!" Mary shouted finally opening her eyes to glare up at him.

"Nothing happened," Ida said as she leant down behind us. "I'll take her upstairs," she continued as she pushed past us and held out her hand. Despite her distress Mary took Ida's outstretched hand and stood.

I stayed crouched in shock, unable to process what had happened as Ida led Mary away. Everyone had stilled, the music had stopped and silently Mary walked from the room. Then the bawd was there, leaning over the bar. "No good you being down on the floor. Leave Mary be, you've got work to do. And you," the bawd said, clicking her fingers at another girl, "get this mess cleared up, now."

"Yes Ma'am," I whispered past the lump in my throat as the girl rushed past me to find a brush. I pushed myself up to standing. As I pulled up some glasses and poured some drinks the chatter started and the piano began to play; within seconds the moment had passed as the thoughts of the crowd had moved on.

Within an hour Ida was back. "She's sleeping," she said as she came up to me.

"I don't understand it, she was doing so well. But then, she's always been with Freda, God only knows what lies she's been feeding her."

"Freda may not like you, and may like Will a little too much, but she's not vindictive, she wants to keep her safe. Anyway, for now she's asleep and we still have work to do," she said before turning to a couple of men waiting at the bar.

As the evening wore on I started collecting the final glasses and tidying the tables. Mary-Jane, who was supposed to be helping me, finally caught-up with me as I was getting ready to clean down. "Clara. I know I was meant to help you finish up tonight but the old bawd wants me to run an errand for her," she said in a rush.

"Now? It's the middle of the night."

"I know." Mary-Jane looked concerned as she bit her lip. "Harry'll be with me though. Look, I'll be fine. Don't wait for me." With that she was gone.

I finished wiping down the bar and as Will walked in I decided to call it a night. Tossing the cloth into the corner I walked to Will where he was waiting for me by the door.

"Have you seen Mary yet?" he asked.

"No and obviously neither have you."

We took the stairs two at a time and ran through the corridors. I dashed past rooms full of overzealous men and overworked women and skimmed past boys looking for their next grind. As we ran up to the next floor it became quieter. The men who came up here were usually regulars, the ones the girls spent more time with, the doors kept closed under more trusted hands. Finally we came to Mary's room.

"Mary." I tapped on the door. "Mary?" I called gently. I eased the door opened and crept in. An oil lamp was still burning golden and low beside the bed, its dim glow barely punctuating the dark room.

I held my hand up for Will to stay where he was. I kept my footsteps soft as I walked to the bed and leant down. Her eyes were closed but her face was pained with dark circles under her eyes that were thrown into sharp relief by the lamps softly flickering flame.

I placed my hand on Mary's forehead, relieved not to feel a fever or cold sweat, before leaving her to her troubled night's sleep. I walked back, waving Will from the room. "She's sleeping," I whispered, "there's no point waking her, it will just upset her further."

Will closed the door and pulled me into his arms. Stood in the corridor of a busy brothel we held one another, surrounded by the sounds of the brothel; men, women, music and calls of laugher rang through the late air.

As the noise faded into the back of my mind Will kissed me, his hands moving to caress my face. He pulled away, pushing his forehead to mine. "I don't know what to do," he whispered.

"For tonight, we go to bed. There is nothing to be done at this hour."

"You're right, you're always right."

Will lead me back to our room where he rolled into bed. I curled up next to him, my head resting on his outstretched arm, and watched him. He lay still, staring at the ceiling, lost in thought.

That night left me agitated and scared as dreams of dense fog and images of Will falling into an endless abyss filled my mind.

I awoke with a start, my breathing heavy, to find Will standing over me already dressed. "I think we should confront her," he said without prelude.

"Okay," I answered slowly, rubbing the night's dreams from my face and pushing myself up.

"After breakfast, see what she's like, get her on her own. No Freda to interfere," he said with obvious irritation. "Then we can talk it through."

"Alright, just let me get my bearings, it's barely dawn."

"I know, I've been awake for hours thinking about it, about her," he said, beginning to pace the room. "To be honest the rest of the house has been a bit raucous this morning, must have had a late one last night."

He pulled me out of bed and stood, twitchy and fidgeting, as I got dressed. He dragged me from the room and through the now deserted house. If we had not been so preoccupied we would have realised just how odd that was. However, blinded by our own distress, we noticed nothing outside of our insular world that, at the time, felt like an all-consuming weight upon our chests.

We ran down the stairs, oblivious to all around us, and hurried down the corridor. We slowed as we came down the basement stairs and walked into the kitchen. We entered a deathly silence. Some of the women were sobbing; others sat clutching one another, trying to find consolation. We walked quietly through the room and took our places at the table. I looked to the bawd, waiting with bated breath to hear what had happened.

"The Butcher has taken another," she announced.

A collective gasp ran around the table. Will's hand reached for mine under the table. As the girls cried the men stared, their eyes wide with a new wave of fear. Will squeezed my hand. I lifted my head to look at him but he was regarding the bawd carefully. My eyes slid over the table until they came to rest on Freda, her face showed nothing but stunned disbelief.

"Mary-Jane was murdered last night. She was stabbed and beaten like the others. Please, let us pray for her s oul," the bawd said.

Her words hit me and my breath caught in my throat, my body frozen. Will clutched my hand tighter. He leaned towards me, he was whispering something, but I could hear nothing. All I could see was the girl's faces. There expressions came to me like the fast moving images of a zoetrope; everything remaining still while the revolving pictures played out before my eyes. The expressions were a mixture of sadness, fear and misunderstanding. I looked again at Freda, her eyes glazed with tears. Suddenly she dropped her head as Will yanked my hand. Ida quickly took my other. As I looked again around the table I understood. I quickly followed suit, bowing my head in silent prayer. I had only known her briefly but could feel the mountain of heartbreak it had given the girls to hear this terrible news. Once we had finished our prayers for Mary-Jane the bawd continued.

"I do not wish to lose another to this monster. As of tonight no one is to venture out alone. We now have Will, who has been taken on as extra security." I shot Will a glare; evidently there was a lot he had not told me. "If for any reason you need to leave the house, you must have either Harry or Will with you. Do you understand?"

We all nodded our assent.

We picked at our food in silence, the house lost in tragedy. The room was plunged into silence. Eventually the bawd cleared her throat. "We cannot allow this Apron Murderer to break us. We will not wilt away, we will not back down. This is our home and we fight for what is ours. I will not see another tear shed nor one more fearful glance. We stay strong, we open our doors to the paying men and we keep with our trade. Now, everyone back to work."

As she stood we got to our feet. Will was immediately hailed by Harry but looked back at me meaningfully; Mary was not here. Before I could say anything Freda called to me and Harry chivvied Will to follow. With one last look back at Will I followed Freda to the bar.

"Ida, you're with me too," Freda called over her shoulder as we left the kitchen, her composure regained, her look of distain back in place. Ida and I shared a curious look as she slowly pushed her seat back, the feet of the chair scraping loudly as she stood, and got to her feet. We followed Freda up the dark, narrow staircase from the basement kitchen and up to the ground floor bar.

She sat herself elegantly on a bar stool and appraised us reprovingly, all thoughts of Mary-Jane pushed from her mind. "Ma'am wants us to up it a bit. You two hav e been getting a few looks round here and people have noticed. The bawd wants you to do a dance for the men," she said, tossing her hair over her shoulder, "you know, give them something else to think about."

I was struck dumb at the idea and then horror stirred within me at the thought of what Will would think. "I'm not entirely…" I started but Freda cut me off.

"Don't start with all that, ma'am says you're to do it, so you'll do it, or find somewhere else to stay. And with that murderer out there, what choice do you really have?"

The Farthing and The Devil

"We know Freda and I don't think that's what Clara w as saying." Ida gave me a quick, cautionary glance before looking passively back at Freda.

"What was she saying then?" Freda asked, chewing her cheek with soured eyes.

"I was saying that I had never danced before. It will take some practice," I said, heeding Ida's warning.

Freda pushed herself off the stall and walked into the middle of the room where she began shifting chairs to the side, making a large space in the middle.

"We'd better get started then," she said leaning forward on the back of the chair she had just moved and smiling slyly.

The dance steps were simple in themselves, but when we put the different steps together with the music I began to struggle. Again and again we rehearsed the dance, Freda playing out a simple tune on the piano while Ida and I tripped over one another's feet and stumbled over the simplest of steps.

"Again," cried Freda in exasperation, "and you spin left not right after the flick Clara."

"Oh, right. I mean left, it's right that it's left," I joked, much to Freda's distain. I heard Ida stifle her giggle in her handkerchief.

"Again."

By lunch I was covered in a sticky layer of sweat but Ida and I had finally managed to get it right for an entire run through.

"Get something down you, you'll be putting on some boots when we get you back."

We met Will in the kitchen already half way through his lunch.

"You had a chance to see Mary?" he asked before I had sat down.

"No, spent all morning learning to dance. What happened to your hair?" I asked.

"Got it cut," he said, running a hand self-consciously through it. Before it had been just touching his shoulders, usually tied back with an old piece of leather, but now it was a mass of black hair spiking in a hundred different directions atop his head.

"I liked it longer."

Will was soon hailed by Harry and he was on his feet and out of the door with only enough time to give me a brief kiss on my cheek. That, unfortunately, also signalled the next round of dance lessons.

As we went from bare feet to boots Mary joined us, sidling into the room like a frightened mouse.

"I thought Mary might wanna join in," Freda announced as Mary gave me a wary look.

"That's great Mary, come over, you'll be fantastic at this," I enthused, trying to mend the rift that had somehow crept between us. "It will be fun, especially now you're here. Here, stand between Ida and me."

"Yes," Ida said giving Mary a sideways look, "then you can be the one to catch her." She raised her brow and gave her a wink and a smile.

Mary said nothing but looked slightly less daunted as she looked at Freda for guidance.

"Well, you've been watching them work, you think you've got the steps?"

"I think so?" she muttered timidly. I looked at Mary questioningly. "I was watching you earlier on, it looked like fun," she shrugged, her shoulders rolling forwards so she looked slightly hunched, her arms wrapped around herself self-consciously.

"Let's give it a go then. One, two three…"

Within hours Mary was beginning to come out of herself. She started laughing at Ida and I as we tripped, fell and generally exasperated Freda. This was something, it seemed, that Mary was naturally good at. She picked up the steps faster than either of us and was soon busy correcting us along with Freda. It had seemed like years but finally I heard her laugh. To see her holding her stomach as she doubled over laughing suddenly made all of our sacrifices worthwhile.

At opening time Harry took his place by the front door with Will stationed by the entrance to the bar. The evening started with men wandering in for the odd drink, mostly to get away from the cold wind that was blowing outside than to find a woman. I smiled and made small talk with the punters, leaving Mary to keep the bar clean and well stocked. As the night progressed it slowly got more rowdy. I kept the drink flowing and as they became more intoxicated I could see them getting freer with their money.

It was just gone ten when I looked up to see the bawd striding into the room, a steely glint in her eye. She dragged over a chair and clambered onto the bar, gesturing for Mary, Ida and I to do the same. With a great sigh Ida and I heaved ourselves up beside her and bent down to help Mary.

The bawd cleared her throat. "Good evening gentleman, may I have your attention please." She held her hands high, waiting for silence to fall. Looking down she nudged a sleeping drunk's head off of the bar with her toe before continuing. "We have an extra surprise for you tonight. Your lovely barmaids have taken it upon themselves to dance for you. Please show them your appreciation!" She ended with a large grin at the crowd that did not touch her eyes but showed her broken teeth in uncompromising lucidity. As she climbed down, her back to the room, she whispered to us, "make sure you do a good job."

All I could do was stare in shock as everyone looked at us expectantly. There was a moment of excruciating silence. Then, with the starting melody from the piano, the music began and I took my first, wobbly, steps of the routine.

I glanced at Ida and could see her doing the same while Mary danced freely, her eyes unfocussed as she twirled, her head tilted back slightly. She looked happier than I had seen her since the night of the attack, but I was unsettled by it, she looked odd as she danced, like she was with us, but not. Her eyes did not look to anyone in particular for support, nor did they dart around the room in fear, she was just, dancing.

By instinct my eyes scanned the room for Will. I saw him stood at the back, on duty, watching me, his back straight and his eyes twinkling under his mob of unruly black hair. As our eyes locked he made an odd gesture with his mouth, pointing at his cheeks. I frowned at him and he shook his head frantically, pointing again at his cheeks and then at me. Finally I understood and I forced a smile onto my face. With the crowds encouragement I slowly began to enjoy myself.

At the end of the dance I took my finishing stance, my hands held high in confidence, a genuine smile lightening my face. The crowd were cheering and as I got down from the bar I noticed they had put tips in a glass they had passed around the room. We had made more money in five minutes than we would have made in a week on the streets.

That evening we performed twice more to copious applause. As the last customer of the night left I closed the door, wishing them a good night and a safe journey home. As soon as the door was locked I flung my arms around Ida and squealed in delight. I had never made so much money in such a short space of time.

"Can you believe it Ida, they liked it, they really liked it!"

Ida wrapped her arms around me, giggling like a small child. "That was so much fun," she enthused.

"I know, and to think, all that work for a few minutes stood on a bar tapping our feet."

"I think you did more than that." Will's deep chuckle in my ear caused a wave of relief to wash over me as his arms wrapped around me from behind.

"And that is my cue to call it a night. Have a lovely evening," Ida said as she stepped back in a vain attempt at restoring her modesty in front of Will.

"You too Ida, good night," Will said leaning forward and giving her a kiss on the cheek.

"Good night Ida," I grinned.

I smiled as I leaned back into Will's arms. I felt like I had achieved something. I was no longer that street girl, selling potatoes and begging for scraps. My heart leapt as my spirit swelled. I looked over to Mary, wishing she would share in our triumph. She gave me a weak smile before turning to leave. I reached out to stop her. "Aww, come on Mary. This is amazing; working here, we are going to do so well. Just look at what we've done since we got here. This is good." Her eyes had lost their faraway look; instead it had been replaced by that glassy stare that fixed on no particular object or person.

She mumbled something unintelligible and walked away, shrinking away from the men as they brushed past her.

I turned, and wrapping my arms around Will's neck I interlaced my fingers, resting the palms of my hands on the back of his neck while my eyes stayed on Mary's retreating form. "I don't know if talking will help," I eventually said. Pulling my eyes away from her I looked up, scrutinising Will's face.

"What do you mean?"

"She's not really here, is she? Not really with us."

"I know," he answered swallowing as his eyes slid to the door she had just walked through.

In the weeks that followed we continued with our routine. It was quickly becoming more popular and soon we had men turning up just to watch us dance. Ida and I lived off the attention, fed off the vibes from the crowds, the comments from the other girls. It made us feel important, like we were part of something, which was something the two of us had searched for for some time. After all, that was how we had become so close, the bar maid and the cleaning maid, both living in the house while not being a part of it. Now we were a crucial part of the brothels entertainment. I only wished Mary felt the same.

One night we were dancing, my head thrown back in laughter as I span, my skirt flying out with my hands held high. Ida was next to me, spinning in time. As the music got faster, more frenzied, we turned faster, keeping up with the unrelenting tempo. I turned; my head whipping to the front, my eyes focussing for a brief moment on the far wall to keep my balance before I span again. The room was a blur of vibrant colour and light as the elaborately papered walls bled into one. I span again and, as I turned, a face amongst the crowd caught my attention. As I twirled again, slower this time, I locked eyes with him.

John was here.

I turned again. He was gone. As I continued to spin I kept looking, trying to spot him in the crowd. Will had begun making his way deeper into the room. I could see him studying the crowd, craning his neck, trying to look where I was looking.

Suddenly he was there; five feet from the bar, four steps from me. I saw him smile as he held something up to the light before throwing it. In the whirl of hair, skirts and mismatched faces I saw the farthing spin and tumble through the air. Arching across the room it turned, catching and reflecting the light as it fell. The small clatter as it landed on the table deafened me, each clunk and click a nail in my coffin.

I looked to Will as John grabbed at my ankle. I kicked him away while trying to keep my tenuous balance. He took a firmer hold as I tried to twist my leg from his grasp. I felt myself stumble as the grip momentarily released and I managed to regain my footing. I looked for Will amongst the crowd; he was shouldering his way towards me now, trying to shout over the music. My hands were thrown out to balance me, trying to hold a hand that was not there. I heard a cry of alarm pass my lips. His fingers wrapped around my ankle again. As the crowd surged I was yanked; I tied to lean back but felt myself tipping towards the crowd. I felt no pain but looked down to briefly see my ankle twisted, the soul still trying to find its purchase upon the bar.

I felt myself falling through the air, my arms flailing uselessly until my head hit the floor. Bright lights dominated my vision, the faces of those above me lost to blotches of light and dark as my mind swam in darkness. As my eyes cleared I saw him. I blinked, trying to clear my vision as panic speared through my chest like a cold knife.

As my eyes refocused I could not see him. I looked into the mass of disjointed feet, bodies and flailing hands. I could hear Will shouting, his voice rising above the din of the crowd. All of a sudden the vice around my ankle disappeared and I felt hands grabbing me by the tops of my arms. As I was hauled to my feet I span to see Will hovering protectively in front of me, the crowd were backing away. My heart stopped as, by the door, I saw him being dragged from the room, his face bloodied. It was John. His eyes not once left my face as, bellowing incoherently, he was dragged from the house.

He had found me.

***

The drums have stopped; the Fa is resting, the village sleeps as the candles burn low. All is quiet at this late hour.

As I sit, the stillness of the hot, dry night silences my tormented mind, John's words from all those years ago echo in my head:

'I'll get you for this, you bitch.'

Chapter 17

As the crowd calmed the music resumed. I turned back to the bar but was blocked by Will.

"Let's have a dance," he whispered, a hard growl governing his voice.

He caught me by the wrist and pulled me towards him. I waltzed around the room in his iron hold, waiting for the crowd to disperse. I could feel the muscles of his back tense under the touch of my hand. He had recognized him as well. I pulled myself against him so we could talk in relative privacy.

"Where's Mary gone?" I whispered.

"She went to bed; she was too upset to stay down here. Freda is staying with her." He stopped to check no one was listening before continuing. "He was watching you, not her, you. You know him, don't you?" He pulled back to look at me.

I dropped my eyes to the floor, not knowing how to respond; maybe my past was not as buried as I thought it was. I closed my eyes and swallowed before meeting his accusing gaze. "He attacked me back in Devils Acre."

He pulled me against him once more. "You never said anything about being attacked. Who is he to you?" he snarled menacingly in my ear.

"You're very cosy, fancy sharing yourselves around?" a voice called from beside us. It was the bawd.

I gave myself a shake, pulling myself back to the present. I released Will. Standing back and taking a breath I walked away to find a client to dance with. Catching Will's eye as I danced around the room I knew we were going to continue our conversation once the bar had closed. I could not relax, as much as I wanted the evening to end, I equally did not want to continue with Will's questioning.

As the evening wound down the last man left. Will followed him out and locked down the brothel behind him. He returned as I was wiping down the bar. My hand froze, mid sweep, as I looked into his wretched face. He had a barrenness to his eyes I had never seen before. He looked desolate; all hope and love seeming to have abandoned him as he walked quietly towards me. I straightened and wiped the last few crumbs from the bar.

"We need to talk," I said as I wrung the cloth I was holding in my hands in the basin.

"Do we?"

"Yes. I need to explain, I need for you to know. I'm sorry."

He raised a humourless brow and stepped back as I walked past with my pail of water. Carrying the heavy basin out from around the bar I abandoned it on a small table.

"Let's talk," Will said, his voice cold.

"Not here," I said casting a wry eye over the bar. I stepped past him and hastened up the stairs. My past was being thrown into my present and I felt lost, lost at sea, caught in a current I could not possibly control and only just treading water, the sullies of my previous life drowning me once more.

I did not stop when I reached the door to our room but flung the door open in a sudden tirade of fear, loss and anger. As Will padded into the room behind me I stopped, my breathing laboured and my heart volatile as my blood thrummed through ears, my temples throbbing in time with the unrelenting beat.

"Who is he?" Will asked quietly, his head down but his eyes gazing up into mine under his dark knitted brows. They were two black pools, the ebb and flow of warring emotions clear in the dark depths.

"He's called John. He was back in Devils Acre. He attacked me," I whispered, my voice only barely audible.

"You knew him, all along, you knew him? Why didn't you say anything? We could have stopped him. You could have gone to the police, but you didn't, you did nothing and now he's back, and Mary, Mary. What were you thinking Clara?" My name was almost a sob that proclaimed his despair. I could hear his agony in the way he dirtied my name, with the bitterness that tainted his tone.

"I didn't think Will! I just didn't think. John was part of my past; he had nothing to do with us, with this."

"He was the one who raped Mary. He raped our Mary. Clara! And you knew him!" Will shouted, his face rife with pain.

"I'm sorry Will." I raised my hands and took a step towards him.

Will raised his hands as he stepped away from me. "I thought we were your family," he said backing up before turning to walk away.

I stood trembling in the middle of the room as the reality of what I had done hit me. My unrestrained breathing became faster as the breath began to hitch in my throat. Tears spilled from my eyes as my hand went to my trembling lips. A desperate cry called from my throat as I backed into the corner. I slid to the floor and wept as shivering heaves of pain rolled through my body. I felt it all, not only the pain I had caused Mary and Will, but the pain of losing Grace, mother and father; the waves of devastation washing over me anew.

Slowly the cold of the wall crept into my bones and as my tears dried I wiped them away from my cheeks with shaking fingers. I pushed myself up and stood in the corner, not knowing where I should go nor what I should do. I tilted my head back and took a deep steadying breath. Mary must be my first priority, she was the one most hurt by my self-centred actions.

When I reached Mary's room I knocked gently. There was no answer. I eased the door open, the tiny creaks echoing through the quieting house. I poked my head around the door and softly called her name. There was no oil lamp burning and no moon shining through the window to give a hint of light. The most I could make out from the light from the hall was the still form of Mary on the bed. With no reply I retreated, closing the door softly behind me. With the door shut I leant my back against it and prayed for forgiveness and divine guidance.

Will did not reappear that night and was not in the kitchen come morning.

"He's already gone. Grabbed what he could and left," Ida said giving me a sympathetic look.

"Yeah, right mighty rage you two had last night, wasn't it, ay?"

"How's Mary?" I asked, choosing to ignore Freda's question.

"Could be better, could be worse," Freda said as she assessed her breakfast muffin with contempt. "You got yourself a lot of trouble on your hands you have." Her small, triumphant smile made my ears ring with fury.

I closed my eyes as I allowed my anger to flow through me until it dissipated to a more manageable level. "I think I'll make an early start Ida, I'll see you upstairs." I took a breakfast muffin as I passed. Slamming the door as I left, rage rolled through me like wild water. Obviously our heated words of last night had whispered their way through the house.

I did not see Will, Mary or Freda until that evening when Ida and I were due to perform. Will stationed himself at the back of the room and kept his eyes on the crowd, doing a constant sweep of the room with his eyes. Mary stayed behind the bar, only serving drinks when absolutely necessary and even then Freda would waltz over to help her. With the bar packed with thirsty men I did not have a chance to speak to Mary alone and over the din of resonating voices a whispered conversation was impossible.

There was no reappearance from John, but the damage had been done. Mary had withdrawn back into her protective cocoon. As soon as the last person left Will went to lock-up for the night and did not return and Mary scuttled off to her room.

For weeks we worked this way, at an impasse of impassable emotions. We wandered through life at the brothel with unspoken words and imperious hurt. The very air I breathed was thick with the bitter taste of remorse which served as a constant reminder of the betrayal I had cast upon the very people I counted as my family.

Will would not speak to me, choosing only to whisper to Mary. His eyes were leaden and guarded whenever I tried to approach and I soon stopped trying, hoping that he would come to me when he was ready. I kept my distance and watched as Freda waltzed around him, smiling as she offered him another drink, her eyes then sliding to me, her arrogant joy taunting me from across the room. I said nothing, but averted my eyes and kept on with my work.

One night I was lost to my nightmares, the unending screams of my sister's agony echoing through my mind, when I was woken by pounding on the bedroom door. I leapt out of bed and before I could make it to the door the hammering began again, this time followed by a chorus of shouting. I struggled into my clothes and flung the door open to find people flying in all directions.

"Quick, the shipment's come early. We have to get it unloaded before dawn," one of the girls said in a panic before rushing away. I presumed I was supposed to follow.

"What's going on? What shipment?" I asked as I ran behind her.

"Just hurry up!"

We rushed into the cold night air and ran through the misty streets. Our shadows chased us, hastening us along as the stars guided us between dark dwellings. The houses towered above us in the light cast by the sharp crescent moon that scarred the sky with its bright slice of light. I looked for Mary but it seemed she had not joined the midnight raid.

We scurried through the streets, darting between hazy pools of cobble, illuminated by the streetlamps yellow glow, our group a mass of gathered skirts and whispered instructions. As we reached the docks a hue of orange was just beginning to streak across the grey sky. Despite the hour the docks were a bustle of activity. The boat was docked at one of the jetties, a ramp connecting it to the shore.

As I reached the ramp a man jogged towards me and handed me a tightly wrapped parcel. This was followed by another and another and another after that. When it was impossible for me to take anymore I was ordered back to the house. I moved out of the way as more girls came forward to collect the illicit goods. I waited for the group to finish being loaded up before leaving the dock. With women being attacked and murdered on an almost a weekly basis and John possibly close at hand I had more reasons than most not to wander these streets alone.

We started making our way back in a silent convoy. We kept to the edges of the streets to avoid being seen from the windows high above. At the slightest sound we would stay, sinking deeper into the shadows, unmoving, until we were sure the danger had passed. Every lit lamp or twitched curtain was a sign of danger, every dark doorway a possible hiding place for John.

Once we reached the house we were told to wait in the alley. We could not attract too much attention to ourselves. Harry let us in pairs and small groups. Once inside my hands were freed from the mixture of odd, cloth wrapped objects. I followed the girls up the stairs and watched as the parcels were passed up into the attic where the hatch was firmly closed behind them.

Too exhausted by the nights events I collapsed back into bed as the sun rose, its bright morning rays glowing through my window. I rolled over and tried in vain to block out the sunrise for a few more precious minutes.

When I could no longer feign sleep I dragged myself out of bed and pulled on my dress. I stepped out of my room, not knowing my destination, and found the hall abandoned. I stood and listened, no floorboards creaked, no laughter called and no angry muttering of discontent rang through the corridor. Either the house was still sleeping or they were in the basement kitchen. As the quietness enveloped me once more, curiosity pulled at my imagination, curiosity of what was behind forbidden doors.

I crept along the corridor and made my way through the house. Eventually I came to the steep, rickety stairs that led up to the attic. They went up every few steps, turning on a tight angle, stopping at a hatch set into the ceiling.

I slowly made my way up, mindful of the uneven footing. As I ascended the stairs I looked back. I was sure I saw a light flicker across the wall, either that, or my guilty mind was playing tricks on me. I waited with bated breath; no footsteps followed the unknown gleam of candle light. I was alone.

Chapter 18

With one last look down the corridor I stepped up to the hatch. Giving it a hard shove with my shoulder it swung up and over revealing nothing but darkness and a dank smell. I coughed as I inhaled the dust. Peering into the darkness I could only make out the shadowed corners of boxes and the slightest gleam of stacked bottles. Jumping quietly down the stairs I slinked to the wall where I reached up and unhooked one of the oil lamps. Holding it up high, like a protective talisman, I stepped into the attic. Rats scrabbled for cover behind boxes and underneath boards as the pressure of my step caused the wood to groan.

I was surrounded by boxes. I leant down and brushed away the thick coating of dust. It was alcohol, the good stuff, not the cheap, watered down brews that were stored in the basement. I scrambled over the cases, innately aware that I was carrying a lit oil lamp over high grade alcohol, and stepped up to the objects of my fascination. They were stacked along the far side of the attic, far out of sight of anyone just poking their head through the hatch.

The odd-shaped objects were wrapped carefully in blankets. They looked so out of place. I stepped up to a pile and tentatively reached out my hand. I pulled back the sheet. The linen billowed silently to the floor to reveal a pile of large, cream-coloured horns. Some were the size of my arm, while others stood taller than me, propped against the wall. I could not place such strange objects in my mind. I studied them, felt the grooves and scores that marred their surface, felt the way they started so large only to narrow to a blunt point at the tip.

Suddenly I heard the creak of a floor board below. Leaving the horns on show, the blanket abandoned to the floor, I scrambled over the boxes and bent down on the pretence of picking one up, the lamp balanced precariously on top of it.

"Clara. What are you doing up here? And what are you trying to do with that? You'll burn the whole house down."

"Will?" I stopped, at a complete loss for words as my face turned towards him.

He scrambled to the oil lamp and lifted it from the box. "You haven't answered my question. What are you doing here?" His face was hard, his jaw tense as he looked at me.

The cold edge that cut his words short made my teeth set and grind. "I could ask you the same thing?" I spat at him after a long silence.

"I was doing…" he stumbled on his words as his eyes flashed from me to the stash of horns, "no one should be up here."

"You knew about this?" I cried incredulously, putting down the box I was holding, my voice rising as anger leeched through my carefully manifested vestige of calm.

"About what? I haven't got time for this Clara. I have a job to do," he snorted as he turned to leave.

"What gives you the right?" I shouted at his back.

He did not turn, but stopped, his foot on the first stair, and tilted his head slightly in my direction. "The right to what?" he asked quietly.

"To judge me," I called through my barely contained sob. "I know what I did was wrong. But to behave like this? To do this to me?" I cried as I stumbled over the boxes towards him. "I'm sorry, alright, I'm sorry."

"This isn't about being sorry Clara, thi s is about Mary, about us." He pushed his hands into his face, kneading the flesh below his eyes. His hands fell to his sides as he turned to me. "We are a family. We're supposed to stick together."

"We do, or at least we did," I said as tears slid down my face. "I was scared Will, it all happened so fast. How did I know it was really him? It could have just been in my head and then I would have dragged up my past, put Mary through more hell than she has already been through, and it would have been for nothing."

"You could have told me." He closed his eyes. When he opened them again he was looking at me for the first time since our quarrel.

"Tell me what is really going on," I whispered.

As Will opened his mouth to speak the echo of a crash rattled through the attic.

"What was that…?"

"We'll talk later, I've got to go," he said looking from me to the hatch. "That could be…" he did not finish his sentence as he ran down the stairs.

I stood for a moment, looking blindly after Will, before I ran. I clattered down the stairs, clumsily pulling the door too behind me, before taking the rest of the steps two at a time. When I did not see Will in the next corridor I ran down the stairs, barely keeping my footing in my haste, my hand skimming over the bannister as though it were made of silk. Running down the corridor, I halted suddenly. I was next to Mary's room. I could hear sobbing from within. Softly placing my hand against the dark stained wood I pushed the door open.

Will was sat on the edge of her bed. I watched as he pulled the hair away from her face and wiped away the tears that were glistening on her cheeks in the dimmed light. As I moved into the room the floor creaked and I heard something grind against the wall. Looking down I saw the remains of Mary's dresser leaning against the wall. As I looked at the room in greater detail I could see the draws had been pulled out and the contents thrown across the floor. The mirror had been smashed, the fragments glinting between the strewn clothing. The dresser's carcass had been pushed over, the corner of it now caught in the wall paper causing it to rip and crumple. I felt a crawling, clawing sensation climb up my back as my mind manipulated the image of the bawd's reaction to the destruction I was staring at.

"What happened?" I asked as I gingerly made my way further into the room.

Mary did not move from where she lay, curled on the bed, her head pressed into the pillow. Will looked from Mary to me; his body hunched, tense, clearly showing what he was trying to hide.

"Mary, did you do this?" I asked, not taking my eyes off Will.

"No no no," she cried, "I didn't do it, he did, he did. He did it!" she screamed into the pillow.

I took the oil lamp from her sideboard and turned up the flame before scraping the debris from the door and closing it firmly. "Who's he?" I asked as I turned back to her, the pain on her face now clearly visible.

"It was him. It was the Devil," she cried, still not lifting her head.

"Calm down Mary," Will soothed while looking to me in alarm.

"What's going on Mary?" I asked, stepping forward.

The room was silent, my question hanging in the air, as slowly Mary stopped shaking. I heard her sobs die to nothing more than heavy breaths. She sat up, looking at us cautiously. "Why did you make such a mess?" she tutted, looking blankly at the destruction that surrounded us.

"What do you mean?" I pressed gently, my eyes sliding to Will.

"Oh, that's right, it was him," Mary dismissed.

"Who?" Will asked, his whole body tensing and coiling once more.

"No one," Mary answered in a sing song voice. She smiled blandly up at Will. "Is the ivory okay? Ma'am wouldn't want it going missing?"

"How did you know?" he asked. I could see him searching Mary's face for the girl who had been with us a few moments ago.

"About what?" She tilted her head, her hair falling across her face in dishevelled locks as she continued to gaze at him.

"The ivory," Will clarified.

"Sorry, the what?" I asked, stepping closer and sitting on the bed.

"The horns, they're the tusks from elephants and the horns from rhinos," Will answered, his eyes still fixed on Mary.

"Next year it's going to become illegal to ship it in," Mary whispered knowingly. "They're stockpiling it here, as well as other places, so that when the supply dries up they can sell it for four, even five times the amount it's being sold for now," Mary continued, her voice rising with every word. Her explanation sounded rehearsed, the words not her own.

Will looked to me and I held his gaze. A wave of fear rolled through my stomach. "Mary, what were you crying about?" I asked my question slowly, so she could not pretend to mishear.

"Nothing. Nothing, nothing, nothing. What do I have to be sad about?" she asked curiously. Her eyes glazed and refocused before looking to each of us, her lids wide, her bottom lip caught under her teeth. Slowly she leaned forward. "I hope nobody saw you," she whispered.

"Saw us? Saw us do what?" Will asked, his expression flitting from concern to confusion.

"The raid last night. So glad you're okay Clara," she said, clasping my arm and smiling slightly.

"Yes, I was fine, we were all fine," I answered, placing my hand over hers and smiling softly.

Out of the corner of my eye I noticed Will still. "What do you mean 'I'?" he asked, his voice losing all the warmth it held mere moments ago.

"The 'midnight raid'. I was woken up last night, got taken to the docks. Had no idea what in the name of the Lord was going on, I just followed everyone else," I half laughed.

"What?" A look of horror crept across Wills face as his body stilled. "You went last night?"

"Yes. Why is that such an issue? If you knew about this you must have known we were going?" I said as I looked to Mary once more.

"You weren't supposed to go, especially not after what happened." Will stopped, unwilling to continue.

"Why?" I asked.

"Third party involvement," he murmured. His lips barley moved as he articulated his concern before sealing them firmly before his gritted teeth.

"And by that you mean?" I prompted, my brow raised at his quiet musings.

"I mean bad people doing bad things," he eventually conceded.

"Nothing bad happened last night," I said, frowning at his evasive answers.

"You were lucky," he stated coldly before is face fell to more dark, brooding thoughts.

"We were well organised," I threw back at him, regarding him shrewdly.

Will gazed at me. I could see his body shift as he weighed up his options, his brows knitted in indecision.

The tension in the room began to build, the air becoming thick and heavy in my lungs. "For heaven's sake Will, just tell me what's been going on," I eventually cried.

"Alright, alright," Will pacified, raising a hand in the darkness to quiet my accusing tone. "I don't know everything, but I know a fair bit," he said, running a hand through his riotous hair. "When we were first taken on here it was for more than one reason. They needed more people for their side business."

"For the ivory?" I asked.

"Yes. But I don't know if the murders are to do with the ivory or the brothel," he said answering my veiled question, "but I wanted you two to stay out of it all."

My eyes fell to Mary; she was humming to herself, an odd, disjointed tune. "So you knew about all this and didn't tell us?"

"I wasn't too worried because you two weren't *working* with the men and had nothing to do with the ivory. I thought I could keep you both here, where you were relatively safe, but still keep you away from the ivory. Then John turns up and all this happens." Will gestured at the two of us. "I don't know what the hell is going on in this town, but I didn't want either of you caught up in it. Now you're both up to your necks in things that shouldn't concern you."

"What do you mean, both of us? Mary, did you know about this?" My eyes flew to Mary before darting back to Will.

Mary did not move, but her eyes seemed focussed on the wall. Now she was listening.

"She's known longer than I have. The bawd has been using her," Will spat.

"What?" I leaned forwards but Mary pushed me away and looked between Will and me defiantly.

"She's not been using me, I've been helping," Mary snapped. "Freda and I have been in charge of keeping count of it all and making sure it all goes to the right place."

"I thought they were stockpiling it here?" Will said, his brows rising to the heavens in unwelcome surprise.

"Ma'am has been pawning it off. People would come and pick it up from the back entrance."

"I would have known if you were doing that," Will said, looking to me for support.

"No you wouldn't. It was when you two were working."

"That's where you and Freda were going?" I asked.

"Ma'am made me promise not to tell," Mary said proudly, "ma'am trusts me."

"It's alright Mary, no one's blaming you for anything, it's all going to be okay," Will soothed.

"Everything's been fine all along. You're just worrying yourself half to death over nothing," Mary clipped, affronted once more.

"Over nothing? Only a few weeks ago Mary-Jane was killed, and before that there was a girl stabbed just around the corner from here," I half shouted.

"I know and I haven't left the house once, the men have always come to me to pick it up."

"Oh right, so they can pick you up and carry you off. At least that way they don't have the trouble of stalking you down some back alley." Will enthused every word with the audacity he felt at her careless actions.

"Stop Will! The bawd was looking out for me."

"The bawd hasn't been our only issue recently," Will sniped.

He was about to continue but Mary interrupted him, "and you can't go blaming Clara either."

"Can't blame Clara? Mary…" Will exclaimed.

"For not saying anything about John," she continued over him. Mary leaned towards me and whispered, "I would have done the same," as a ghostlike smile played across her lips.

"But why are you so upset?" Will asked.

Mary shook her head. "I'm not troubled by that."

"About what then?" Will pressed.

"Nothing, I'm upset about nothing." I could see the curtains being pulled behind her eyes. We had gotten too close, pushed her too far. "I'm feeling tired now." Her eyes glazed over and she began humming again as she lay down and pulled the covers up to her chin. "Night then."

"Alright," I said patting her knee, "sleep well." I knew there was nothing to be gained from trying to force Mary into anything; she would just shut herself off, retreat deeper within herself. "Let's leave her to rest," I whispered to Will.

As we walked down the corridor Will took my hand. I leant into him and he released my hand, wrapping his arm around my shoulders, pulling me in close to him.

"We'll be okay, we'll make this work," he said as he pressed his lips to my temple. "We have to, Mary needs us to."

He led me to our room where he sat on the bed, still agitated, his elbows on his knees, his hands never still.

"So, that's it. Mary has a mad turn and suddenly we're alright?" I laughed un-humorously as I paced the room.

"No, it's not. Look," he said, "I'm sorry for the way I've acted and for the things I've said, but you've got to see that you were in the wrong. You should have said something, if not to Mary, then to me."

"I was. I was wrong." I wrapped my arms around myself, picking at a small patch of dry skin on my forearm. "Will, I was scared and frightened and confused and, and, I don't know. It was like my life before I met you and my life now were colliding."

"It's the same life," he said, his hand reaching out to me.

"No it's not."

"That's what Mary says, and what do you say about that?" he asked, his hand stopping before my arm and falling to the bed.

"I know, but I don't want my old life destroying what we've built, what we've scraped together. Not after everything we've been through."

"That old life's never going away Clara; it's a part of you, just as my past is still a part of me. It's what's made you who you are today and it's the reason you've survived this long. It's not that distant, if it was you wouldn't have the nightmares."

"You're right. I…" I stopped, unsure what to say. I took a breath. "What are we going to do about Mary?"

"I don't know." I saw him look at me questioningly, but with a tense edge to his eye that made me stomach drop. "Maybe it's worth speaking to Freda."

"And maybe we could announce our problems to the entire brothel," I snorted, flopping down next to him. I stared up at the ceiling, at the patches of damp and cracked plaster.

Will eventually gave a hollow laugh. "She may not like you particularly, but she likes Mary. She'll want to protect her. I'll talk to her tomorrow when I sort out that dresser."

"Good luck explaining that one."

"I'll just say Freda had a rowdy one last night, things got out of hand, happens all the time." I felt him shrug indifferently.

We lay in silence for an age, both lost in thought.

"I missed you you know" I whispered into the darkness.

"I missed you too," he gently laughed as he rolled his head to the side so he was looking at me. A small, restrained smile was pulling at the edge of his mouth. Slowly he pressed his lips to mine, the moment marred only slightly by the discomposure between us.

Chapter 19

The months passed cold and dark. There were more murders, more stabbings, and rape was becoming a constant bone of contention within the local brothels. The streets were more dangerous than they ever had been. As the attacks became more frequent and started to get closer to home we realised no one was safe. Whatever evil was surrounding Whitechapel, it was quickly closing in on us.

Mary, despite our talk that night, had isolated herself from us completely. Will and I were alone, sat at the kitchen table, hurriedly eating an early supper. I took no notice of the clatter of someone coming down the stairs until I saw Will stop, his spoon stilling in his bowl of broth, as his eyes fixed on the other side of the room. I followed his gaze to where Freda had walked in. She did not look to us as she leaned into the linin basket by the door, collecting fresh bar towels. Her back stiffened and, despite turning slightly to pick up a dropped rag, she did not acknowledge us.

"How's Mary?" Will asked.

I saw her arms still before she half stood and leant her hands on the edge of the waist-high basket. With all her weight on the hamper she turned her head to Will and me. "She's fine. Just like she was the last time you asked."

"Will she be joining us tonight?" I asked brightly, forcing a smile onto my face.

"No, she don't feel up to it."

"Has she eaten?" Will interjected.

"Yes, she's eaten, as I promised you'. But like I said, she don't want to see nobody. She needs rest."

"Freda…" I stuttered.

"I gotta go." Freda pulled herself up, using the wall to brace herself, and left the room.

I turned back to Will. "We need to do something."

"I know. I just don't know what we can do." Will rubbed his hand over his face, pushing his hair out of his eyes. "I just wish she would come out of that room. All she does is sit up there and brood. If we knew what she was brooding over? I mean, she's always been able to talk to us, always, about anything."

"I know," I sighed, taking his hand in mine. I turned my face away and caught sight of the clock. "We have to go."

Ida was already working behind the bar when Will and I got there.

"Where were you?" she asked as I came around the bar.

"Sorry, we lost track of time," I said, still distracted as I watched Will's retreating back.

"Mary?" she asked, her eyebrows raised, trying to catch my attention. "Still no change then?" she continued when I did not answer. She sucked on her top lip, catching it between her teeth as she studied my face.

"No, no change." I shook my head and was about to continue when I was distracted by Freda. She was working the tables, but holding onto the back of the chairs whenever she could.

Ida followed my gaze. "She had a rough night. Apparently Harry had to get involved, the guy got kicked out but not before…well, you can see how she is."

"Why is she working?" I said, looking at Freda who was gingerly sitting on a customer's lap.

"She doesn't want to disappoint the bawd. Between you and me there's a bit of discord." Ida gave me a knowing look before lifting down a crate of alcohol and restocking the shelves.

"Why?" I asked as I grabbed a few bottles myself. I knew why. Will had gone to the bawd and told her Mary would not be running the ivory accounts anymore and would do no more backdoor trading. The bawd had not taken the conversation too well. Despite this, I wanted to know what the story was between the girls.

"Haven't heard a lot, just the odd rumour." Ida eyed me suspiciously.

"Don't look at me," I laughed as I pulled down two glasses and served the customers in front of me. "Two of the same?" I asked holding up the glasses. His wink told me all I needed to know.

I did not have another chance to question Ida as the evening dragged on and then it was time for us to dance.

"No sign on Mary again," Ida whispered as we climbed onto the bar.

I shook my head but said nothing as the music began.

So much had changed, not just with Mary, but with the whole brothel. It was no longer a carefree home where the men came to forget their problems; it was a safe house for the women, a place to hide from the shadows that sleuthed through the streets at night. No visitors lingered at night, not anymore. After hours the piano stood silent and the glasses sat on the shelf, polished and shining, the doors stayed locked. The bolts were drawn and the curtains pulled. The women scurried about the house, there shadows flickering on the walls as the scampered between windows, their lanterns burning low.

I was wiping away the last rings of residue from the bar when Ida caught my eye. She smiled and waved her hand in the general direction of the privy as she left the bar with another girl. Nobody went anywhere alone anymore, not even to the outhouse.

I joined Will at the door and we made our way to the upper floors, passing small groups of young women also on their way to bed. As we walked down the quietening corridor we could hear movement behind closed doors, though now it was different. Where once we would hear a man's urgent plea of ecstasy, or a women's laugh at a poorly told joke, we now heard locks clicked, bolts scrapped and chairs jammed against doors. The girls were terrified, no one was safe and there seemed no end to the murderer's rampage.

My retrospection was interrupted when I heard a faltering step behind us. Will turned and pulled me behind him, but almost immediately relaxed his stance. Freda was slowly limping down the corridor.

"You look worse than you did earlier," I said taking a step towards her.

"You know me, couldn't resist a bit of extra bread and honey." She winked knowingly at me as she continued towards us, determined to hide her grimaces of pain.

"Have you seen Mary yet?" I asked.

Freda looked at me carefully, deciding how to answer. "Checked on her earlier. She's alright," she said as she continued past us.

We stood and watched her make her slow progress up the corridor. "Shall we ask if we can see Mary?" I whispered to Will.

"Can't hurt," Will shrugged. "Freda!" he called.

"No," she answered, her hand resting on the handle to Mary's room. "She'll be sleeping and I need my rest and all." She glared down the corridor at us. "Goodnight," she said pointedly.

I took a deep breath, forcing the air through my nostrils as I turned and smiled at her. "Good night Freda, send Mary our love."

Freda rolled her eyes before letting herself into the room and closing the door.

"Well, that went well," Will said, still looking bemusedly at the closed door. I heard a faint rattle and click as the lock was drawn. "I'll talk to her tomorrow," he continued as he ran his hand over my shoulders and pulled me close, kissing the top of my head.

Over the next few weeks the house continued on its decent into darkness. The curtains remained closed and the doors remained locked, only to be opened to hurry known members into the house during trading hours. Mary had stopped coming out of her room altogether. She would only speak to Freda, and she was giving nothing away. A heavy atmosphere hung over the house. The air was thick with fear and the cold mist of dread hung in the air.

Will slammed his fist on the table, making the diners jump. "My apologies ladies," he said to the table at large before turning back to me and continuing our whispered argument. "What do you expect me to do? I have tried talking to her; she doesn't want to talk. I have tried reasoning with her; she won't listen."

"We can't just sit back and do nothing though."

"I'm not saying we do nothing, I'm just saying that I don't know what to do. Look, this problem isn't just between us anymore. The other girls have noticed and the bawd has run out of patience."

"What do you mean?" I asked, my voice low, knowing I would not like the answer.

"It means that we stay here as long as we work and Mary isn't working." He took a long drink before finishing, "I mean she's going to be out on the streets."

"But she can't, not now, not with all this going on. It'd be a death sentence," I whispered urgently, my hand grasping my cup and pressing it to the table to try and steady the shake of my hand.

"My point exactly," Will answered draining his glass, his eyes not moving from mine.

"I'll take her some food and try to get through to her," I said rising from my chair and collecting a tray. I felt the eyes of everyone in the room follow me as I filled it with food.

"Good luck," Will whispered as I gave him a swift kiss on my way out of the kitchen.

I made my way up to her room and knocked on the door. There was no answer. I knocked again, refusing to be ignored. Grabbing the handle I turned it gingerly. It was stuck. Giving it a small shove with my shoulder I realised it was not jammed, it was locked. I placed the tray on the floor and pulled a grip from my hair. Using my teeth I straightened it out and inserted into the key hole. It took me a while to get the lock open; it was only a recently acquired skill from a very dubious Harry, and one I was not well versed at. Eventually I heard a light, satisfying click. With only a second of indecision I rammed the door with my shoulder, bursting into the room.

I stopped. Staring into the darkened room I waited for my eyes to adjust. Mary was lying in her bed, facing away from me. All I could hear was her laboured sobs and my heavy breathing. Leaving the tray outside I paced slowly into the room. After staring for a moment at her still form I sat gingerly on the bed. Resting my hand on her shoulder I took a deep breath, choosing my words carefully.

"Talk to me Mary, please. Tell me what's wrong."

"Just go away. I don't need you, I don't need anyone. I can deal with this on my own." She had her head buried in the pillow, the blankets pulled up to her neck. Her legs were drawn up to her chest, like a small child trying to shut out the world.

"Deal with what on your own? You know you're not alone," I soothed, trying to break through her cracked glass exterior.

"I am. It doesn't matter, no one can help me. Please, just go," she cried as she drew her legs in tighter.

"I am not going anywhere until you talk to me," I said, settling myself deeper onto the bed.

"I said GO!" Mary screamed. Rolling over she pushed me away with her feeble strength before falling to more helpless sobs.

"Come now Mary. Will and I, we're here for you. Whatever it is, we can get through it. But only if you let us help you," I said as I drew her into my arms. I smoothed her hair with my hand and began to rock her gently.

Gradually her sobs subsided and she lay in my arms. "Hush now, shhh, shhh," I lulled as I continued to rock her, continued to hold her. Slowly I felt her muscles release there tension. Her hands had worked their way to me, her fingers wrapped in my shawl, pulling me close to her. I sat with her, held her, as she lay against my body.

"I'm pregnant," she whispered into the darkness, her face pressed against my chest. I could feel her tears seeping through the cotton of my dress.

I stilled as her words sunk in, and I knew.

"It was him," she breathed; every word costing her great pain. "What am I going to do?" she asked slowly, deliberately, infusing every word with her agony, her bloodshot eyes boring into mine as her tears fell like acid, burning away her hope.

"We tell Will," I said, pulling her close once more.

I sat with her as I rocked and softly sang. While on the outside, to Mary, I looked calm, on the inside I was in turmoil. I had no clue as to how Will would react nor what we would do. As the evening wore into night I felt Mary's body slump and relax completely as she drifted to sleep in my arms. I sat, unmoving, holding her close.

There was a soft knock at the door. Looking up I saw the outline of Will leaning through. As he stepped into the room the floorboard creaked, rousing Mary. I felt her stiffen once more as she realised Will was with us; she shrank away, recoiling deeper into herself.

"Go back to sleep Mary, I'll talk to him," I whispered as I shifted her back onto the bed and covered her over with blankets once more.

I walked towards Will. At the door I pressed my hands against his abdomen but he resisted the gentle pressure, refusing to back out of the room. "Mary?" he asked.

"Not now, we need to talk." I saw him look from me to Mary. "Not here," I said, following his gaze, "just, not here." I dropped my head and walked around him, stepping out of the room.

He followed a few seconds later. I said nothing as I walked to our room. The corridors were deserted, the women in bed, drifting in and out of uneasy dreams. I could imagine them stilling in their beds as they heard our tread on the floor, no other sound but their terrified breaths as they waited for us innocent ghouls to pass.

I stepped into our room and closed the door as Will walked in behind me.

"So?" Will said.

I could see him repeatedly fisting and stretching his hands. The silence stretched on.

"Mary's pregnant. By…by….him," I stated.

Will's mouth moved, opening and closing several as his face lost all colour. Running his hands over his face he pushed them deep into his soft pliable skin, the tips of his fingers digging into his eyes, rubbing them to oblivion.

"Is she alright?" he asked eventually, his voice strained.

"What a stupid question," I cried before I could stop myself. I fell silent, considering my words before continuing. "She, I think she's okay, all things considered," I said, staring at a patch of black mould growing on the wall.

"Well," he stated, flicking his fingers nervously one after the other in quick succession. "This is going to take some sorting out." He lapsed into silence and began prowling around the room. Eventually he stopped and looked up. "Stay here, I'll be back. Just give me some time." Without further discussion he turned and left the room, closing the door with an unsettling snap.

I stood in the room, alone. The silence was deafening as I stood, waiting. I was staring out of the window, at the rows upon rows of houses and factories giving a mingling of peeked and square shadows below the dark blue sky. There was a rumour of dawn in the horizon. A light mist hung over the city, a whisper of the clouds that sat high above us during the day.

Dawn was just breaking, a lone black bird calling to the new day's sun, when eventually Will stepped back into the room. He said nothing as he walked towards me. He stopped and leaned over, turning up the oil lamp that was barely burning. I watched as it turned from a muted orange glow to a bright fiery sun that lit the room with its delicate flames.

Will grasped my hand and pulled me to the bed. He sat beside me and took my hand in both of his, still silent. "I've spoken to the bawd," he said. Clearing his throat he continued, "I…you and Mary." He stopped again. "You and Mary are my family," he said, looking into my eyes. "I'm sorry." He lifted our interlinked fingers and rubbed his thumb over my knuckles before bringing them to his lips. "I've got to marry Mary."

"What do you mean?" My hands hardened in his grasp as the air solidified in my lungs, my heart recoiling from his words.

"It's the only way. It's the only way the bawd will allow it. I won't have her killed, not like that girl, not because of this."

I knew he was thinking of the girl in the room. Memories of her dead body flooded my mind until suddenly it was Mary lying prone on the table, her hands falling from her swollen stomach to hang limply from the sides of the table.

"Clara? Did you hear me?" Will had slid himself off the bed and was kneeling in front of me.

"Yes. Yes I heard you," I whispered, my voice broken. I freed my hands from his firm grasp and wiped away the tears as they began to fall. "I understand."

I sat and stared at him, watched the tears pool in his eyes as he gently closed his lids and restrained his emotions. I leant forward and pressed my lips to his as a sob broke through the tumour in my throat. Leaning back again I took in a harrowing breath and smoothed down my dress, pushing out invisible creases.

"We need to tell Mary," I chocked as I pushed myself to my feet.

"Clara…"

"I know Will."

Slowly, I made my way to Mary's room, Will walking in my wake, silent.

Mary was still on her bed, the blanket still draped over her body. Her breaths were slow, like a calm swell; waves moving in an endless sea; on the surface she appeared tranquil, concealing the dark and dangerous currents rolling beneath. I stepped quietly into the room and sat on the edge of her bed. Will stood beside me. Bending down he gently smoothed the hair from her face, bent, and kissed her head.

I closed my eyes, allowing our situation to wash over me, as I took Mary's hand and said a silent prayer.

Epilogue

An inconspicuous cough at the door invades my solemn thoughts. I drop my pen, quickly close the book and pull the cloth over the leather surface. Taking a breath I push myself back in the chair as my heart sinks. Remembering that night, the night we discovered just how lost Mary, was my body trembles; the pain as sharp and searing as it had been that day.

"Are you ready to go?" he asks.

"Almost," I cough, as I clear my throat of untamed emotion.

"Do you think it'll get there?"

"Yes," I say, unequivocal in my answer.

"Do you really think it's worth it?" he asks. Not waiting for my reply, he leaves me once more.

"It has to be," I whisper, "I have no time to finish." My voice is lost to the empty hut.

Freeing my journal from the cotton once more, I tear a piece of the parchment away from the back page and scrawl a note before I give it to the Captain:

> *This is all I have time to write. More will follow.*
> *I promise, you will know the truth.*
>
> *Clara x*

I close the old, leather-bound book and run my hands over its soft cover. Rising from my chair I go back to the cabinet and pull out a roughly rolled piece of twine and my small knife. I walk back to the table, unravel two lengths and cut it to size. I tie my journal closed and, lifting it to my lips, step out of the hut.

I stumble through the soundless streets. The frenetic beat is now no more than distant memory, the dancing men lost in their lucid dreams. My heart pounds on, now beating to a rhythm of its own; my throat constricts with the deep pain of loss.

I wind my way through the small village, passing silently by the earthen huts; my legs following a familiar path. My bare feet scrape the dark, dusty ground, now cool in the light of the moo n. I welcome the relief from the burning sun that bleaches the bark, scolds the leaves and bakes the soil. All appears burnt under the endless blue expanse that stretches above us from dawn to dusk.

For now the sky holds nothing but the stars. Billions of distant lights blink at me from a land much greater than this mortal plain. I walk, still gazing into the dark, endless abyss overhead, until I feel my toes sink into moist powder. I have come to the river. A cool breeze calls over the water. I close my eyes and inhale the moist air, hugging the journal close to my chest, close to my heart.

I pad softly into the shallow water, until I feel the wooden gang plank against the soles of my feet. I tread gently upon the wood, feeling it bend under each footstep, before stepping onto the boat. I ignore the sailors as they jostle me from side to side and walk across the deck to where the captain is standing, giving orders to his men.

He turns to me; his cap pulled low, his pipe drooping from the corner of his mouth. "Th is it then?" he asks, holding out his hand.

"Yes, this is it, for now at least," I mutter haltingly as I hand over the package.

"I see," he mutters past his pipe as he peers at it through the layers of skin that surround his face.

"Please…" I begin.

"It'll get there," he wheezes, pulling heavily on his pipe. "Off you get now. It's time to cast off."

I stumble back, unwilling to turn away, until my legs hits the side of the boat. I turn and find the gang plank. I stumble back to shore where I stand, my shawl pulled tight around my shoulders.

I hear the wood groan and the water murmur as the vessel moves to leave. With a fresh gust of wind the sails fill; the fabric billowing and bowing at the force, the ropes holding fast the rigging to the mast. The boat glides silently over the inky water.

I watch the vessel sail into the darkness, gilded by the bright, iridescent moon that reflects off the rippling water.

Lightning Source UK Ltd.
Milton Keynes UK
UKOW02f2331010515

250782UK00001B/106/P